Phil Bradley's Snow shoe Trail

Silas K. Boone

Phil Bradley's Snow shoe Trail

CHAPTER I — INTO THE LAND OF THE MOOSE AND CARIBOU

"That cold chicken Mrs. McNab put up for our lunch yesterday went fine, fellows; and I only wish we had the like of it for to-day!"

"You always did have a weakness for fowls, Ethan."

"Just so, X-Ray Tyson; that's why they put me out in the left garden on our Brewster baseball team so I could gobble all that were knocked that way."

"Well, we've heard you boasting lots of times about that wonder of a rooster you've got at home."

"Oh! you mean old Robinson Crusoe, don't you, Lub?"

"Yes, that sorrel-topped ungainly looking crow-factory we've all seen strutting around your yard so often. I never ran across an uglier bird, for a fact, if you'll excuse me for saying it, Ethan."

The boy who answered to the last mentioned name only laughed as he continued:

"No apologies needed, X-Ray; because I know myself he's sure no beauty; but say, let me tell you he's a scrapper from the ground up."

"How on earth did you ever come to call him by such a queer name, Ethan? Did you happen to get him on Friday? Mebbe you found him on an island; or fished him out after a shipwreck on the water?"

"You're away off your base, Lub. I'll proceed to enlighten you a bit. It's a wonder to me some of you haven't asked about that before now. First of all, we got him from a man named Robinson, who peddles chickens, and collects eggs through Brewster territory. For a while we always referred to him as 'Robinson's fowl.' Get that?"

"Yes, but go on, Ethan."

"Well, when he had his fierce fight with Zack Avery's game rooster that had beaten everything to flinders, and Robinson actually whipped him, we began to think he deserved a medal. After he had made the game run for home he perched on the dividing fence and let everybody know about it with his clarion voice; so I said right on the spot he ought to be given the rest of the famous Robinson name because he crew so!"

"Oh! somebody take hold of me, or I'm liable to fall off the sled and be left behind!" shouted the boy called Lub, and who was well named it appeared, judging from his generous proportions.

The stout boy was duly restrained and hugged by X-Ray Tyson and Ethan until he begged his companions to desist.

"I didn't mean that I wanted you to squeeze me to death," he complained; "that would be jumping out of the fryingpan into the fire. I'm fully recovered now from my weakness: but, Ethan, please don't do anything like that again."

There were just four boys in the party, all dressed warmly for a winter outing, and perched upon a number of bundles that went to make up the cargo of the homely old Canadian two-horse sledge, built not unlike those in common use around Moscow during a Russian winter.

Besides Ethan Allen, X-Ray Tyson and the stout youth, Lub Fenwick, whose real name however was Osmond, there was a fourth lad, to whom the others seemed to defer in a way that might suggest leadership.

In fact Phil Bradley did occupy this position among his chums, and with reason, for none of them could compare with him in concocting clever ideas, and also in carrying out the same.

They all belonged to the town of Brewster, which was situated hundreds of miles to the southwest of where we find them on this crisp winter day.

Those who have had the opportunity of reading the earlier volumes in this series know how it happened that there was no school in session in Brewster that fall and early winter, so that the scholars were given a long vacation.

3

Phil and his three chums had come to call themselves the Mountain Boys; just why we have not the time or space to explain here, except that it may have had something to do with Ethan Allen's ancestors, who were Revolutionary heroes, and connected with the famous Green Mountain Boys.

Phil was an orphan who had been left a large fortune in trust, so that he could do almost as he liked financially; though he had no bad habits, and used his means in a healthy way for the benefit of others, as well as his own enjoyment. Lub had a rich aunt who spoiled him; and the parents of the Tyson boy were also considered well-to-do — by the way his name was really Raymond, but he was always so quick to see through things, that his playmates soon corrupted his first name as above.

These four boys were ambitious to take certain trips calculated to call for considerable expenditure of cash. The Allens, not being rich, and Ethan, being too proud to accept of continuous favors at the hands of Phil, for a time it looked as if the magic combination must be broken.

Between them the other three hatched up a wonderful scheme which they immediately put into operation. It has been spoken of in earlier books, but in order that new readers may understand the situation, a few words of explanation may not be amiss.

Ethan had always been a boy given to earning various sums of money by doing odd jobs, and at the recommendation of Phil he started to use some old traps he happened to own, with more or less success in securing such pelts as muskrats in the marsh, together with an occasional fox or mink, while even 'coons yielded up their hides for his benefit.

In the spring and summer Ethan scoured the woods for certain valuable roots such as wild ginseng, golden rod and others. These he dried, and when he had a quantity, shipped to a certain dealer according to the directions of Phil.

4

The results were certainly pleasing, for the checks that came back made Ethan very proud. But the fact of the matter was, this was all a little scheme of Phil's. To tell the truth the pretended dealer in roots and furs down in New York was a certain rich bachelor uncle of Phil's, who entered heartily into the game, once he learned the purpose of his nephew's idea.

He even had letter heads and envelopes printed as though he might be doing a land-office business in purchasing such commodities. But if the wonderfully fine prices that he paid Ethan for everything he sent prevailed all along the line, it is likely that nine-tenths of the male population of the country would be turning their attention to such profitable pursuits.

Of course the reader can understand that nine-tenths of the money Ethan received in these complimentary letters came from Phil; but not for worlds would this intelligence be allowed to reach the proud trapper and root-hunter.

It was in one way rather a mean thing to do, but the intention was noble. It allowed Ethan to pay his share of the general expenses on their outings, and saved his self-respect. Granted that he never learned of the subterfuge everything would be well.

There were times, however, when Ethan quite naturally boasted just a little about his superior ability to dry roots better than anybody else; and also of his grand luck in trapping a prize black fox, when in reality the skin that brought him almost three hundred dollars was not worth more than five at the most.

On these occasions Lub would titter a little, though he quickly turned it off if Ethan turned to stare at him, by coughing, and complaining of a tickling in his throat.

Only when they were positive that Ethan was out of hearing did the three conspirators dare compare notes on this subject, and laugh over the success of their grand scheme. But as X-Ray once said, it was like skating over a "ticklish bender" on the frozen mill pond; because they might try it once too often, and excite the suspicion of the boy who was being hoodwinked, greatly to his profit.

Phil and his three chums had spent some time in camp up in the Adirondacks not a great while back. Their latest trip had been down on the Coast along a certain section on Currituck Sound, where Phil owned a "shooting lodge" that had been left to him by an old hermit. What amazing adventures developed during their stay on the salt water in pursuit of wild fowl have been given in detail in the preceding volume.

This trip up into the Canadian wilderness had been planned for a long time. In fact ever since X-Ray received a present on the last Christmas of a pair of fine Canadian show-shoes he had done little but talk of his desire to some time or other get up there where they always had plenty of snow, just to learn how to use his treasured gift.

Strangely enough there had never come about a time since then when he could do any decent work with his snow-shoes. When a fall of snow did come along it was followed by a soft spell that ruined the going; and so it came about that here they were, headed for a certain place in the Canadian "bush," where they hoped to spend a week or two hunting, and enjoying themselves in every possible way.

Phil had been put in touch with an old Scotch farmer who had promised to take them bag and baggage into the woods, and come for them again at a certain date. On the previous morning they had started over the snow on his queer sledge, with a large quantity of luggage that was intended to make for their comfort. One night they had camped on the way, and "The" McNab, whose other name was Tammis, promised that before darkness rolled around again he would have them located in the best hunting region of the Saguenay country.

Of course X-Ray Tyson was not the only one who had snow-shoes, because there were three other pairs in plain sight. Phil alone really had had previous practical experience on the clumsy "gunboats," as Lub called them; though X-Ray claimed to have paddled around in his yard many times on an inch of snow, without any dire disaster.

The McNab was a red-faced Scotch-Canadian, warm of heart, though possibly a bit over fond of imbibing, and perhaps not as dependable as he might be when in one of these bibulous moods.

He was greatly interested in the four lively American lads, and listened to the many stories they told connected with their past experiences.

Thus the second morning of their tedious ride began to wear away. Surrounded by the rough country that characterizes all this section of northeast Canada, they began to feel that ere long they would be cut off from all communication with civilization.

All that morning they had not seen a single house of any description. The road over which the two sturdy Canadian shaggy ponies were dragging the sledge was only a logging or "tote" road along which teams sometimes went on the way to or from some logging camp situated nearer the river.

"We'll soon be leaving even this road, and taking to the bush, you say, Mr. McNab?" Lub was asking, as he clutched the arm of Ethan in a sudden spasm of fear lest he be shaken from his seat when one of the runners of the sled struck an obstruction, tilting the whole load dangerously.

"Oh, aye, but I assure ye it couldno' be any worse than this. Ye ken that the road is seldom used, and it gets in a peetiful state. But it will not be for lang. When we turn off the going will be better, ye understand."

Mr. McNab had a very broad touch of the brogue. Lub loved to hear him roll the "R's" off his thick tongue, and often asked questions just to be amused in that way.

"Look ahead there, will you?" cried out X-Ray just then; for when it came to using his eyes to advantage the Tyson boy had all of his chums "beaten to a frazzle," as Ethan used to say; "here comes a man walking along the road. Why, we must be getting near a town of some kind."

7

"Aweel, laddy, nae doot ye think so, but it taks more than one man to mak a toun. That party is a logger coming from the camp. I dinna ken why he should be giving up his job so airly in the season, but it may be he is seek, or has had some sorry news frae hame."

The brawny logger had an ax, with a small bundle suspended from the same, slung over his shoulder. He stopped and waited for them to come up, when he nodded his head in salutation.

"You're The McNab, I take it," he remarked, addressing the driver of the shaggy ponies. "I'm one of the Sawyer bunch over on the river ten miles away. On my way back home; wife down with a fever and the kids need me. Get up later on if all goes well. What sort of a crowd are you taking up into the bush this time, Tammis? Seems like a young outfit for such big game hunting."

"Oh! ay, so it does," replied the driver, quickly; "but these braw laddies hae seen muckle mair o' such business than most men that come up this way. They weel know how to tak care o' themselves, nae doot. What are the chances for game this season; and do ye know o' anny ither parties in the bush?"

"I hear there are moose aplenty this year," the logger replied, as he filled his pipe from the bag of tobacco McNab held out to him; "and so far I've only heard tell o' one party o' sportsmen along these parts. They're camped nigh the Hogback on Cranberry Creek."

"Seems to me I heard talk aboot the Baylay coming back to his old haunts again. They did say he had reformed, but, mon, they leed, fo' that de'il would never be annything but the toughest man in all the Saguenay region, though he lived to a hundred."

"Yes, they say it's true, and one of our crew ran across him," the logger returned, with a frown, and a shake of the head. "He is still nursing a broken head; and bore the word from Baylay that if any other loggers tried to take the quarrel up they knew where to find him."

"Oh, ay, he never hides his light under a bushel, mon. And I only hope that the laddies here will not run a foul of the braggart while they are in the bush."

"Well, if they do they'd better knuckle under, and whisper small. There isn't a man I know as would be willing to stack up against Baylay when he's roused and in one of his quarrelsome moods. He is a terror if ever there was one. But I must be on my way; the sooner I get home the better. Good-by to ye, boys, and I hope ye have a fine time; but beware Baylay!"

He struck out down the logging road with his bundle dangling from the ax that lay across his shoulder. McNab chirped to his ponies and once more the sledge started on its way.

Lub had an apprehensive look on his chubby face. His eyes sought those of Phil in a mute inquiry.

"Would you mind telling us something about this man, Baylay, Mr. McNab?" asked Phil; while both X-Ray Tyson and Ethan nodded their approval, for their curiosity had also been aroused.

"Oh! ay, though the least said aboot him the better," replied the driver, as he glanced uneasily on either side of the road at the thick "bush" as though he half feared lest the party under discussion might be within earshot of them and take offense; "he is a verra big and powerful man who has a most ungovernable temper. He has gi'en the authorities a great deal o' trouble in the past, but it is maist difficult to get any one to try and arrest him. He has been a logger in his time, and one o' the best ever known along the river. They say he used to smuggle across the border; and to this day he kills game out o' season as he pleases; yet the wardens are sore afraid to attempt his arrest."

"Whew! that sounds nice, I must say!" exclaimed X-Ray Tyson.

"Rather an unpleasant neighbor to have around, seems to me," added Ethan.

"I should remark," declared Lub.

9

"I only hope," Phil finished with, "that we don't have the bad luck to run across this Baylay while we're up here. For while it might be policy for us to knuckle down and try not to cross such a quarrelsome man, it goes against the grain of the Mountain Boys to be meek and uncomplaining when they are in the right."

"That's what we all say, Phil!" declared X-Ray.

Tammis McNab looked at his charges, and rubbed his bristly chin reflectively, as though it struck him there might be some lively times in prospect in case these American lads and the Baylay did happen to run up against each other in the bush.

CHAPTER II — BESIDE THE FRAGRANT CAMP FIRE

"I heard say that this Baylay had come back to his old haunts; does that mean he used to live up in this section, Mr. McNab?" asked Phil, a little later, showing that his thoughts were still fixed upon the unpleasant neighbor they were likely to have during their outing.

"Aweel, he did spend some time up aboot this way," the driver replied. "You see, the mon has a family, for all his wild ways, and somehow he manages to support the wife and childer and a raft o' dogs, though it's a mystery how he does the same."

"Children you say, and up here in this wilderness?" exclaimed Lub, looking more or less surprised.

"Oh! ay, a pair o' thim I'm tawld, tho' for the matter I couldno' say for certain, since I never ha' set eyes on the same. They tell me that the wife is a wee sma' woman, but that she has been known to subdue her giant husband as no mortal man ever dared."

"Gee! I'd like to see her do it, then," asserted X-Ray, impulsively, of course never dreaming at the time that any such opportunity would drift his way.

When noon came they stopped and made a fire, so as to have hot coffee, which of course every one declared to be very refreshing, for they were chilled more or less by the long inaction.

Then it was on again deeper into the wilderness. The road had been abandoned for some time, since it turned sharply in the wrong direction, heading for the lumber camp on the river. Besides, the vicinity of such a place, where trees were falling all day long, and rough loggers calling out or singing at their labor, could not be reckoned a good hunting-ground, since the game would be scared away.

As the shadows began to lengthen the boys were cheered by hearing Tammis declare they were now close on the spot he had in mind. Once before some years back he had piloted a hunting-party up here, and from

11

all accounts the prospects for big game were much better this season than for a long while back.

One of Phil's hobbies was along the line of flashlight photography. Indeed, he had become quite fascinated with the idea of "shooting game with a camera," and was even losing some of his hunter spirit that had until recently been such a pronounced part of his make-up.

He had already made quite a collection of wonderful pictures, and yearned for other worlds to conquer. Some of these days he declared he meant to take a trip into the fastnesses of Darkest Africa, where he could snap off the wild animals in their native haunts—elephant, lion, rhinoceros, hippopotamus and every other species of creature that lives in jungle and swamp and forest in the country which Roosevelt had recently visited on his great hunt.

Of course Phil expected to add to his collection while on this jaunt; and since Ethan was a born hunter, with X-Ray backing him up, they could supply the camp with what fresh meat was necessary, leaving Lub to manage the culinary department, and lend Phil a helping hand if necessary.

The sun was just about an hour high when McNab suddenly drew in his shaggy team.

"What mair cud ye want than this braw place, laddies?" he demanded, as he sat there, and swept his hand around in a semi-circle.

Phil followed his movement. He saw that indeed there could hardly be a finer spot for camping. It was on the shore of a lake, and they could look far out over the ice-covered surface to where the fir crowned hills came down to the further shore, fully a mile away.

Situated in the heart of the virgin forest, with the ax of the logger still a stranger to the splendid growth of timber, it seemed to offer them a glorious opportunity for spending their fortnight there in the wilderness.

The boys jumped to the ground, and commenced exercising their arms so as to induce a better circulation of blood.

"No need of that, fellows," laughed Phil; "we're going to have plenty of things to do to tire you out before we get settled here. Grab hold, and unload the sledge to begin with. Then all of us must get busy putting up some sort of temporary shelter for the night, like we did before. To-morrow we can start in to build a more permanent one that will resist a blizzard if it comes along."

McNab looked after his team while the Mountain Boys began to get to work under the direction of their leader; for Phil happened to know a great deal more about this sort of thing than any of his three chums.

The merry whack of the two axes they had fetched along told that preparations were underway looking to the temporary shelter spoken of by Phil. Lub was quite an adept in building fires for cooking purposes, since he had had considerable practice; accordingly no one interfered when he started to roll two logs he had picked out until he had them forming what might be called a V, with a little space separating the ends that were close together.

In arranging this he had made sure to leave the broad end toward the prevailing breeze, which at the time was from the west. This insured a good draught, once the fire was lighted; and would also conduce to the comfort of the cook bending over the coals, as it would blow the pungent smoke away from his face.

Phil, not knowing what they might strike away up in this section of Canada, had made sure to purchase certain supplies at a sporting goods emporium in New York, and which had come to him through the mails. Just what these were none of the other boys knew up to the present, though Phil had promised to tell them before long.

Of course they had coffee and tea, sugar, biscuits, bacon, salt pork, beans, rice, some canned goods and like things. And at McNab's they had been fortunate enough to lay in quite a supply of butter and fresh eggs, that might last through half of their expected two weeks in the woods.

By the time darkness began to gather the shelter for the night had been completed, and they clustered around the fire intending to take things easy, as well as eagerly sniff the tempting odors that were beginning to permeate the neighboring atmosphere.

"Now is the chance to tell us, Phil, what under the sun you have in that big package you got from New York City before we left home," suggested X-Ray, who did not like to have anything that was connected with a mystery go long unexplained.

"Well, I suppose I had better keep my promise," laughed Phil, starting to cut the cords that bound the package in question; "or else you will have a fit. There never could be a secret when you were around."

"Oh! I don't know about that," muttered X-Ray, giving Phil a wink, and then looking blandly toward the unconscious Ethan who did not dream that he was concerned in the matter in the least.

"Well, these are some of the concentrated foods that are used by prospectors and Arctic explorers, who can carry but a small pack on their backs, and yet may starve to death for all the game they can get. They are splendid in their way, I'm told, though I must confess that outside of the condensed milk and the soups I never tasted any of these things. I know what they are, though."

The boys commenced examining the various articles for themselves.

"Now tell me what the dickens erbswurst can be?" demanded Ethan as he took up a strange roll that must have weighed several pounds, and looked like a sausage.

"Oh! that's in common use in Germany, especially in the army. It is made of concentrated pea-meal ready to use, and with other vegetables, and some dried meat mixed in with it. You can eat it as it is, or made into a soup it is very fine, and will sustain life better than almost any other thing you could find."

"And what is this queer looking can that has a label telling that it is self-heating; explain to me how can that be?" asked X-Ray Tyson.

"That is really a wonderful discovery, and duck hunters shivering in their blind, on a winter morning, balloonists far up among the clouds, and all persons who need something warm to take away their shaky feeling, but can't have a fire, find a great boon in those soups."

"But how can it be self-heating I'd like to know?" asked Ethan, scornfully.

"It is after all very simple," explained Phil. "The soup is in a second can, and the space between the two is filled with dry quick-lime. When wanted, a small hole is cut in the top of the outer can and some water allowed to pass in. This you see generates a terrific heat, and in a jiffy the soup is made piping hot."

"Well, did you ever hear the beat of that?" exclaimed Lub, who had stopped his culinary labors long enough to look and listen to what was going on, for it really concerned his department.

"And here we have some desiccated vegetables, looks like," remarked Ethan, as he pointed to a variety of cans.

"Those are what they call dehydrated vegetables," explained Phil. "They are potatoes, spinach, onions and cabbage in a concentrated form. One can weighing from four to twelve ounces is equal to from seven to fifteen pounds of the fresh stuff."

"But how do you use them?" asked Lub, wonderingly, thinking no doubt what a labor saving device this would be for the cook.

"Oh!" Phil told him, "just add the proper amount of water to a small portion, and cook it the same way you would the fresh vegetable. They are used pretty generally in the United States navy, I understand; for it is

15

sometimes hard to get green stuff, and a diet of salt meat is apt to induce scurvy in sailors."

"Well, I see you have soup tablets," continued X-Ray Tyson, examining still further, "something that is called trumilk, and another that goes by the name of truegg; do you mean to tell me these are all right, and that you can actually carry eggs along in powder shape?"

"Yes, two of those cans of condensed eggs are equal to four dozen of the fresh variety," explained Phil. "They say they are fine, scrambled or in omelettes, and that is the way we can use them after our other supply gives out."

"Well, if only you've got the money to buy things," remarked Ethan, "there's no need of anybody going into the woods, and taking chances of starving these days, when they supply all these wonderful condensed things. But as for me I'd rather just keep them for an emergency, and live on the fat of the land as long as I could find any fresh meat."

The old Scotch-Canadian was greatly impressed with the explanations given by Phil. He examined the various cans and packages closely, and seemed to handle them almost reverently, as though it was utterly beyond his ken how they could so preserve eggs and things in such a condensed form. And yet for years he had been using, off and on, milk that had been conserved after the same principle.

"Supper's ready for serving, fellows; so get your pannikins where I can dish things out!" announced Lub about that time.

They were soon enjoying themselves about as well as any one could wish. Really Lub was getting better at his profession all the time, and X-Ray as well as Ethan did not hesitate to tell him so.

"Now, I know you're just giving me that taffy so as to influence me to keep on the job right along," urged Lub, a little suspicious when the "Greeks came bearing gifts," though his eyes did twinkle with gratification at hearing the warm praise, because time had been when the same fat boy was very green in connection with camp cookery, and afforded his chums many a hearty laugh over his blunders.

"Honest to goodness I mean every word of it, and more too, Lub!" affirmed X-Ray.

"I never tasted a better cup of coffee," declared Ethan; "and these beans are warmed up to beat the band; while the bacon is as crisp and brown as — well, as I could fry it myself, and that's the highest praise anybody would want to have handed out to them, I guess."

There was enough and to spare, for after the last appetite had been appeased Lub declared that it was a shame to leave that small portion, so he would have to put it away himself, which he accordingly did, though they warned him he was in danger of bursting from over feeding.

Afterwards they made themselves comfortable, each with his warm blanket about his shoulders, and facing the fire. A couple of logs rolled up near the blaze afforded them seats, and for at least two hours they continued to chat on every sort of subject.

Their home life was often touched upon, as well as previous outings in which they had taken part. Ethan even told "The" McNab what wonderful success he had had in his root-gathering and fur-trapping. On hearing how a single black fox skin had netted him three hundred dollars the Scotch farmer said he did not doubt it as he knew a man who had received three times that sum for an especially fine pelt.

"As for meself," he added, "it's verra curious but I never even saw a black fox in all me trapping experience. They do be verra rare, they tell me. I have a good woman and three bairn at home, and a thousand dollars would be a muckle fortune for us, but I dinna expect sich luck to come my way. Ye are verra fortunate I must say, Ethan, lad."

Of course Lub had to titter at that, when X-Ray gave him a kick on the sly, as if to warn him to behave himself, so that their great secret might not be endangered by Ethan having his suspicions aroused.

Presently Lub began to yawn and stretch at a great rate. That might be taken for a sign that he was becoming sleepy, and wanted to turn in. They had their several places portioned off under the temporary shelter, so that if Lub chose he could crawl in when he pleased.

He was evidently of a mind to do so, and had even started to rise to his feet, when the others heard him give vent to an exclamation.

"Didn't that logger say Baylay owned several dogs, fellows?" he demanded.

"Why yes, he did," replied X-Ray, quickly; "but what makes you ask such a thing as that, Lub?"

"Because I reckon then he must be somewhere around here right now, for there's a strange animal nosing about in the shadows over where I threw what scraps were left of our supper!"

At that every one looked. Sure enough they could see a moving figure, that did look like a pretty good-sized dog.

Phil, however, uttered a low word of caution.

"Sit tight, everybody!" he hissed, "until I reach out and take hold of my gun!"

"But, Phil, go slow if that's one of the poacher's dogs!" warned Lub in alarm.

"Dog nothing!" came from Phil as he took up his gun; "that's a gray wolf I tell you!"

CHAPTER III — FISHING THROUGH THE ICE WITH TIP-UPS

No one moved after that save Phil himself, though Lub breathed very hard, as if the information had given him the "heart-jump," he often spoke about.

Phil knew he had made no mistake when he pronounced the prowling animal a bold timber wolf; though he would have had some difficulty in believing it if some one else had told about one of those animals daring to venture so close to a camp where a number of hunters were sitting about a fire.

He judged that the beast must be unusually hungry, or else not in fear of mankind, from some reason or other.

"Whoo! see his green-yellow eyes, will you?" whispered Lub.

"Put the bullet square between 'em, Phil!" advised Ethan, secretly wishing it had been his rifle that was within easy reach at the time.

Hardly had he spoken than there came the report. A jet of flame spurted from the end of the leveled gun; there was one sharp yelp and that was all.

"You got him, Phil!" shouted X-Ray Tyson, always the first to see things that happened.

"Hold on, don't rush over there till you get your guns!" advised Phil. "If the wolves are that brash up here, there may be more of the lot."

McNab had thrown some small stuff on the fire so that the flames shot up, and in this way illuminated the vicinity. They could see a dusky figure sprawled out where the animal had been crouching and glaring at them with his terrible wolfish eyes.

So when Ethan and X-Ray had secured their rifles, with Phil they advanced to the spot where the victim of the shot had fallen. Phil was a trifle concerned himself, and anxious to make certain. If after all it turned out that he had shot a cur dog belonging to that terrible poacher and one-time logger Baylay, it was going to make them a tremendous amount of trouble.

He was speedily convinced, however, that there could be no doubt; and was also rejoiced to hear McNab declare:

"A fearsome sicht I ken, lads, and the largest wolf I ever saw in all my days in the bush. It was a braw shot ye made, Phil; it goed close between the eyes, and finished the beastie for a'. I tauld ye there was game worth the hunting up this way; if only ye may not have the misfortune to run across yon de'il o' a Baylay and get his ill-will."

They stretched the defunct wolf out, and Lub stared at his size, as well as his ferocious appearance, shuddering as he fancied what a time any one would have if attacked by a pack of such monsters.

"I expect I'll let you fellows do most of the prowling while we're up here," he remarked, with the air of one who knew when he was well off. "I never did care very much for that sort, you know; and there will be plenty of things to employ my time around the camp, I guess."

"Yes," Phil told him with a smile, for he knew that Lub's heart was not the most valiant in the world, "and the first chance we get to-morrow I mean to show you how to fish through the ice out there."

"Oh! I've often read of that, Phil, and wished I could have a whack at it," the fat chum exclaimed, rapturously; "please tell me how it's done, won't you? They have what they call tip-ups, I believe, that let them know every time a pickerel takes a bait."

"It's all as easy as falling off a log," Phil went on to say. "You cut half a dozen holes in the ice some little distance apart. Then you drop your baited hook down, and fix a little contraption across the hole, connecting the line with the same. The idea is that when you get a fish his struggles tilts a stick, and lets you know about it. Sometimes one man 'tends dozens of holes, running this way and that as he sees he has a catch, to take the fish off, and rebait the hook."

"Are all the tip-ups alike, Phil?" asked the deeply interested Lub.

"Not by any means, although they have the same common idea of notifying the fisherman that he has made a catch," the other continued. "Some I have seen consist of a stick, with a cord and a red piece of cloth; when the fish is caught he drags on the extra cord, and this causes the flag to appear at the top of the stick set upright in the ice. That is a good way, though it means considerable labor fixing your poles."

"Tell us the easiest way, then," said Lub, who did not care for too much work, because, as he often said, of course in fun, he was "dreadfully afraid of wasting away to just skin and bone."

"The simplest tip-up," said Phil, "consists of a crotch with two short prongs and one longer one. The line is tied to this in such a way that a jerk causes the longer prong to dip down into the hole, though the crotch cannot be wholly drawn through, care being taken to have it too large for that. Of course this tells the watchful fisherman to hurry his stumps and take his catch off."

"Show me how to cut one of those same crotches the first thing in the morning, will you, Phil?" asked Lub; "while the rest of you are building our shack I might as well busy myself out there on the ice gathering in a mess of pickerel and pike, for I reckon both of them live like cousins in our lake."

Phil accordingly agreed to this, and so Lub presently crept off to lie down in his selected place. They heard his deep breathing shortly afterwards, and knew he had passed into the land of dreams.

"I hope Lub doesn't get to hauling in big fish while he's asleep," complained X-Ray Tyson; "I've known him to do the silliest things in his dreams, and it wouldn't surprise me a bit to find him trying to hug me in the night, under the belief that he had hooked a monster sturgeon or muscalonge that was trying to get away from him. If you hear me let out a yell, pull him off, boys, please."

Of course both Phil and Ethan promised faithfully that they would accommodate him, though possibly they were half hoping something of the sort might occur, because it would be a ludicrous sight to see Lub with his arms wrapped around the more slender comrade, who would be gasping, and trying to break away.

"There, it was certainly a wolf let out that wailing howl!" declared Phil, as they were about to follow the example of the fat chum, and crawl into their already arranged blankets.

"Ef I had a bawbee for every one o' the creatures I've heard howl I'd nae doot be fixed for life," The McNab assured them.

"Then it is a wolf, a genuine one, that howled, is it?" asked X-Ray.

"Hoot mon! it could no' be annything else."

"Would they dare attack your ponies, Mr. McNab?" continued Ethan.

"I dinna ken, laddie; but the baith of them have been accustomed to takin' care o' themselves ever sin' they were knee-high to a duck. I would peety the wolf that was brash eno' to tackle the heels o' my ponies."

The thought appeared to amuse McNab, for he continued to chuckle for some little time after he had snuggled into his waiting blanket.

It was a long night, yet nothing happened to disturb the campers. Phil slept in what he was pleased to call "detachments"; that is, he would lie there for an hour or so, and then raise his head to listen, perchance to crawl noiselessly out from his snug nest so as to place more fuel on the smoldering fire; and then under the belief that it would keep going for another spell again seek the warmth of his covers.

At last came the peep of dawn in the east. Phil saw it first, but he did not immediately arouse the others, for they were in no especial hurry, and his fellow campers seemed to be sleeping so soundly it was a pity to disturb them.

Indeed breakfast was well on the way when Lub came crawling out, blinking his heavy eyes, and looking as though he had only burst the bonds that fettered his senses with a great effort.

"What's this I see and smell?" he exclaimed in a voice loud enough to awaken the Seven Sleepers. "Gone and stole a march on me, hey? Got breakfast started, and without calling on the head chef either? All right, go ahead; if I see you making any amateurish mistakes pardon me if I correct you. We want things done according to Soyer's Cook Book in this camp. That's what I'm studying at home, you know. He's simply great. F'r instance, when he starts to tell you how to make rabbit stew he says: 'First, get your rabbit! See how pointed his directions are? Now a lot of cook-books ignore that fundamental condition altogether. They seem to think rabbits grow on bushes, and all you have to do is to put out your hand and pull one in. First get your rabbit! That's sound common sense for you!"

The others began to make their appearance and by the time breakfast was fully prepared all of them were ready to do justice to the spread.

"Are these real eggs, Phil, or the sawdust kind?" demanded X-Ray.

"Well, that hardly needs an answer," he was told; "they may be able to condense eggs in a small compass like dust, but no man who ever lived could put them together again once they are broken, and the yolk runs into the white, Didn't you learn that 'all the king's horses and all the king's men, couldn't put Humpty Dumpty together again'? which meant that it was an egg fell from the wall."

After breakfast McNab hitched up and said good-by to his boy friends.

"Depend on it, laddies," he said, after shaking each one by the hand, "if so be ye dinna arrive at my h'use in twelve days I'll be for startin' up this way once mair till fetch ye back. That is the compact I make ye this day. And the best o' luck be with ye, amen!"

They were sorry to see McNab go, for he was good company; but there was plenty to engross their full attention. Ethan and X-Ray had already begun to use the two camp axes, and the merry sound of their lusty blows was as music to the ears of Phil, who soon had a picture of Camp Brewster in the making, to add to his collection.

Then there was Lub who had hurried through the clearing up of the breakfast things in order to get at that fishing through the ice. They took a hatchet with them so Phil could cut the first hole. After that he showed the fat chum just what kind of a crotch to select from the scrub growing near the shore, and how to fashion it so that it would answer the purpose.

"If we had live minnows I think it would be much better than this bought bait that is said to be extra good for pickerel fishing," Phil told him; "but we couldn't very well fetch such things away up here. Where fishermen make this ice fishing a regular business they keep a big supply of minnows in a spring hole that does not freeze over in winter; and each day they use a quantity until all have been put on the hooks. I don't know much about this patent bait, but it is said to answer a long-felt want."

Lub worked industriously indeed. When he had six good tip-ups made he proceeded to cut five more openings, about fifty feet away from each other. Then he began to bait his hooks, and set the lines.

Before he had the third hook baited he was thrilled to discover the first tip-up trying to get into the hole; and when he saw it moving he hurried over to ascertain whether he really had caught his first fish, or if it was going to turn out a false alarm.

A vicious tug at the line assured him he had something worth while at the other end, and hand over hand Lub pulled a wriggling captive in, finally tossing out on the ice a pickerel weighing at least seven pounds.

No wonder he gave a shout of joy and proceeded to dance around, holding up his glittering barred prize. The others called out to congratulate him on his work. "Do it some more, Lub, and we'll have all the fish chowder we can eat!" Ethan told him; whereupon the delighted fisherman once more started in to finish his line of holes through the ice, working with a will.

The fish must have been pretty hungry in that Canadian lake, or else the "bought" lure that Phil had fetched along with him had some magical properties about it to attract the finny denizens. Certainly they kept Lub hopping from one place to another, amidst frequent bursts of joy, and also considerable puffing; for it must be remembered that the boy was excessively fat, and this action made him short of breath.

The results must have gladdened his heart. Every time he took a pleased look at the stack of fish he had started to build he chuckled with pride and glee. Some of the prizes were by now frozen, and remained where he had placed them; later arrivals flopped all around on the ice; but as fast as they became numb with the cold Lub would add them to his pile.

Such splendid fishing he could not remember of ever indulging in before. After such glorious success the boys would have to crown him as the king of tip-up fishermen. And no doubt Lub's mouth watered as he contemplated the feast that would come at the end of that wonderful day.

If this good luck was going to be a specimen of what was coming their way surely the Canadian trip must be marked down with a red cross in the annals of their vacation experiences.

Lub was wholly given up to his work. So engrossed did he become in it that even the sound of the axes, and the voices of his chums failed to draw his attention any longer. In fact, he was fascinated with the charm of hauling in those glittering striped prizes; with an occasional muscalonge as well, fierce fighters that struggled madly against being dragged from their native element.

The boys ashore had apparently cut enough small trees by now to satisfy their present wants. They no longer used the ax save to trim some end as they started to build the shack.

Phil had put all other things aside, lending his aid to further the work and really things were commencing to look like business.

Ethan and X-Ray were bending down, and urging a stubborn tree trunk to settle in its appointed place, while Phil waited to fasten it there, when without the least warning they heard a wild whoop.

It came with such astonishing vigor that every one of the three boys started up, the business in hand forgotten for the moment.

Of course they knew that it came from Lub out there on the ice. He had been giving some fancy exhibitions of shouting from time to time; so that the others had reached a point where they only grinned on hearing his notes of delight.

But this was different.

There was no chant of joy about the howl that had just reached their ears, to thrill them through and through; on the contrary plain fear dominated the outburst!

CHAPTER IV — LUB'S BEAR

"It's Lub!" exclaimed X-Ray, like a flash, for he was always quick to jump at conclusions.

"He's fallen in one of his holes!" gasped Ethan.

"Not much; it's something worse than that!" cried Phil, as another whoop came to their ears.

It happened that they could not see out on the ice where they were standing, and consequently the first thing any of them thought of doing was to jump around the patch of bushes so as to get a clear view.

They could hardly believe their eyes. There was poor Lub trying his level best to run over the smooth ice, with a shaggy black bear in hot pursuit! Even as they looked the animal went through a queer sort of gymnastic performance, as though striving to seize hold of some object that Lub seemed to be dragging after him.

"It's a fish on one of his lines the bear wants!" exclaimed Phil, hardly knowing whether to burst out laughing, or consider the situation a serious one for the terrified boy on the ice.

He compromised matters by darting aside and snatching up his rifle; an act that caught the eye of Ethan Allen, and was instantly copied by that wideawake individual.

"Help! make him let up chasing after me!" shouted Lub, as well as he was able, considering the fact that he kept slipping and rolling over, only to scramble wildly to his feet, and start off once more in his clumsy fashion.

"Let him have the fish you're dragging after you!" shouted Phil, even as he began to move out on the ice, with the other two at his heels.

"I can't! Line's got fast to my leg; and he ate up all the others anyway!" Lub called back, as he waddled along with frantic zeal.

"Turn to the left so you'll be out of range when we shoot!" bellowed Phil.

Apparently the fugitive heard this, and also understood, for they could see that he was doing his best to obey; though the slippery ice did play all manner of tricks with those uncertain "pins" of his, causing him many a frantic struggle.

As he ran Lub could not keep from "rubbering" as Ethan called it. He would twist his fat neck around in order to learn just how close his hairy pursuer chanced to be at the moment. This helped to make his flight more uncertain, and brought about his downfall several times.

As Phil and Ethan were much more surefooted than the stout boy, and not at all frightened, they made better progress. On this account they gained continually, so that when Lub had managed to sheer off, and presented his left side to them, they were really close enough to make sure of the bear.

"Ready, Ethan?" called out Phil.

"Yes!" came the reply, as both of them suddenly stopped short.

The two reports sounded almost as one. Lub gave another squeal as though his nerves were strained to the limit; but when on casting one of his apprehensive looks over his shoulder he saw his tormentor struggling there on the ice as though he had received his death hurt, the fat boy's humor changed.

"Give him some more, fellows!" he shrieked. "The glutton! to devour all my fine fish. We'll make it up by feasting on bear steak to-night, then; that's the only way to get even. Oh! he's getting up again, and he's got it in for me because I said that. Shoot him once more, Phil!"

"It's no use, because he's done for," Phil told him, for the bear after that expiring effort had fallen back again, and given his last kick.

When Lub made sure of this, and saw that his chums were all gathered about the fallen animal, he summoned up enough courage to join the circle.

"How did it happen, Lub?" asked X-Ray, who had now joined the rest.

The stout chum rubbed his chin, and shrugged his plump shoulders.

"Gee! but he did give me a terrible shock!" he remarked, as though once more passing through the dreadful experience of the surprise.

"Tell us about it," urged Ethan; "and how did it come you let him eat up all your fish without giving the alarm?"

"Well, this is about the way it happened," Lub began. "My back was turned on the pile of fish for I was fighting with the gamiest one of the lot, this husky muscalonge here, the only real decent one that's left," and he mournfully surveyed the still flopping fish that he had been dragging after him all the while.

"Yes, go on, what happened then?" continued the eager X-Ray.

"Why, I remember hearing some sort of champing sound back of me, but I guess I must have thought you fellows were making it ashore. Anyway I never bothered paying the least bit of attention to the same but kept on fighting this musky here for all I was worth. Whew!"

"You pulled the fish in finally of course?" said Ethan as the other paused to wipe his streaming forehead for all it was so cold.

"Yes, with a great big yank," Lub explained. "It kind of flew through the air a bit, and I turned at the same time to see that bear rear up on his hind legs and do his level best to grab the flying fish. When it fell to the ice he started for it, and that was when I managed to let off my first whoop for help."

"Yes, I kind of thought you called out that word, but I wasn't dead sure," X-Ray told him; "but what next did you-all do, as our old friend Simon Blodgett down on the Coast would say?"

"What, me? I ran like everything, fell down, got on my feet again, and seeing the bear putting after me I kept agoing and awhooping for all I was worth."

"Did you know he was after the fish, and not you?" asked Phil, secretly amused, though managing to keep a straight face.

"Why, yes, I got on to that wrinkle, all right," replied the other, "because I could see him trying to fall on the fish every chance he had. But I objected to turning over my last catch to the old scoundrel; even if the line hadn't gone and got fast to my leg I don't believe I'd have let him have it, unless it came to nip and tuck with me."

"Well, you have plenty of time to gather another lot of fish, Lub," suggested Ethan; "and after all, your adventure has been the means of gaining us our first fresh meat in Canada. We paid enough for our licenses to hunt up here to want to get the worth of our good money."

"And, Phil, don't you think I've got a right to call him my bear?" asked Lub, as if struck with a sudden inspiration.

"What! after the two of us shot him?" ejaculated Ethan.

"But didn't I lure him along with my trailing muscalonge?" demanded Lub, triumphantly; "if it hadn't been for me fishing so industriously out here on the ice, and tempting Bruin to show himself, would you have had a chance to shoot? I guess not. You only finished my work for me; I must have had him all tired out running."

Ethan wore a wide grin by that time.

"Sure you did, Lub," he declared frankly, with a wink toward Phil; "anybody could see that you meant to wear him down to his death. His tongue was hanging out of his mouth, and if you'd kept him going long enough there isn't any doubt but that the poor thing would have turned up his toes without a single shot being fired. We'll call him Lub's coaxed bear after this."

"There's two of your tip-ups acting crazy, Lub," called out X-Ray just then; "and you'd better be taking off the fish you'll find on the hooks."

"Isn't this the greatest sort of sport though?" said Lub, as he started off to attend to his lines.

"It certainly couldn't well be beaten!" admitted Phil, as he and his two comrades indulged in a fit of laughter that was none the less vigorous because they chose to keep it silent, out of consideration for the feelings of their beloved fat chum.

"I wonder how it comes this chap hadn't gone into winter quarters yet?" Ethan remarked, poking the dead bear with the toe of his boot. "Down our way they can seldom be seen after the first snowfall, and never come out until there is a regular break-up of winter."

"Well, away up here the winter lasts much longer, and that would account for it," Phil suggested. "They may want to stay out to the very last, knowing how it holds on away up to May. But no matter what the cause, this fine fat fellow stayed out too long."

"He'll not hibernate any more if we know it," observed X-Ray Tyson, with a satisfied smirk; "instead he'll help to fill up four hungry chaps I happen to be acquainted with. And after all what nobler end could any bear wish to come to than that?"

Two of the boys returned, to get busy again on the shack; while Phil stayed out on the ice to attend to taking the hide from the dead bear, and securing what choice portions they wanted.

It promised to be a long task, but Phil did it, as he was in the habit of doing everything he undertook, with exactness. Lub kept on taking more fish, though whenever he found a breathing spell between bites he would amble over to watch what Phil was doing, and make remarks.

"I'll have that skin made into a fine rug, some of these days," he declared, as he ran his hand over the silky hair; "and every time I look at it I'll remember what a great time I had luring the beast within range of your guns."

"What would have been your plan of campaign, Lub, in case we had not happened to be within hailing distance?" asked Phil, looking quite innocent as he said it.

Lub gave him rather a suspicious glance, and then replied loftily:

"Oh! I don't know. To be frank I hadn't reached that point. Mebbe I might have used my knife, and cut the fish line, so he could grab the muscalonge. Then while he was devouring that I might have found a chance to sneak up behind and finish the rascal with one sure blow from my trusty hunting knife. Course I don't actually say I would have done that; but it might have occurred to me, you know."

When Phil allowed his memory to go back and recall the look of terror he had seen on Lub's white face he decided in his own mind that there was about as much chance of such a wonderful feat being carried out as there was of Lub developing wings and flying.

"You're getting as many fish as we can well use, I reckon, Lub?" he remarked, to change the subject.

"Sure thing, Phil; and after I pull in three more I think I'll call it off for to-day. I've covered a good many miles, running from one hole to another, and back again over the whole line. I didn't come up here to reduce myself to a shadow, you know. Over-work is a bad thing for a growing boy, they say."

"There's only one thing I'll always be sorry for, Lub."

"You mean about this bear adventure, don't you?" asked the other, suspiciously.

"Yes. I should have kept my wits about me and have done it, too."

"What was that, Phil?"

"Snatched up my camera and managed to snap off a picture of how you lured your bear into the trap. Some of our boy friends down Brewster-way would like to see it. They may be inclined to doubt more or less when they hear the story; but that would be proof they'd have to accept as genuine, Lub."

The fat boy seemed to consider it for a brief time.

When he turned to meet Phil's gaze again there was a whimsical expression on his face that spoke volumes.

"Well, on the whole, Phil," he went on to say, "I guess I'm just as glad you did forget to grab up your camera that time. You see, in telling a story a fellow might accidentally embellish just a little more each time; and a picture is a terrible accusation, for it keeps you pinned down close to facts. There, I've got a bite on two lines. Whoof, hold on!"

CHAPTER V—X-RAY STRAPS ON HIS SNOW-SHOES

Long before evening came around Lub had time to recover from his excessive labors of the day, so that he was in good trim to start supper.

"It wasn't so much the strain of fishing, and attending to half a dozen tip-ups that knocked me out, as that warm little dance the bear led me, you see, fellows," he explained, when some one chanced to remark that he got up on his feet as though his knee-joints were stiff and rusty.

"Yes," said Ethan, drily, "this thing of luring is always hard on the muscles and nerves. Only the most rugged constitutions can stand it."

Lub grinned, but did not pursue the subject any further. He was soon busily engaged in cooking the fish which had been cleaned and prepared long before.

Luckily they had two good-sized frying-pans with them; for that was one of the occasions where they came in handy. Nothing would do but they must have some bear steak, though Phil warned them they were apt to find it rather tough. Still, who would have the heart to complain about a little thing like that, when the game had fallen to their own rifles, after Lub had gotten in his fine work; certainly none of the Mountain Boys, who had gone through too many episodes along these lines not to accept things as they came, with a laugh and a good word.

That was a bounteous feast, and one to be long remembered. The fish tasted as sweet as shad, and had the same sort of "pitchfork" bones in them too, which must be watched for, and jealousy guarded against. If the bear steak was hard to masticate, at the same time it was a camp dinner, not one served on a damask tablecloth, with cut-glass, and silver, and napkins to boot!

"Well, it's coming along at last, fellows!" announced X-Ray Tyson, about the time they had finished their meal.

"What's that you're referring to?" demanded Ethan; while Lub looked hastily on all sides of him, just as though he half expected to see the mate of his bear standing there on the border of the camp, and sniffing at the odor of cooked meat that still hung around the scene.

"Why, don't you see 'em trailing down?" demanded X-Ray, who seemed to be quite jubilant over something or other.

"He means it's commenced to snow!" said Ethan.

"Just what," the other added, "and if it gets a good move on perhaps to-morrow will see me gliding along on my snow-shoes that I've owned nearly a year now, and never had a decent chance to use."

He made a dive over to where the said articles were hanging, and taking them down proceeded to try them on. The others had seen X-Ray do this so often that it was no novel sight to them.

Phil, who had had considerable experience with snow-shoes, had shown the other some little "wrinkles" in connection with fixing the clumsy contraptions to his feet, so that X-Ray was quite proficient, so far as that part of it went.

He seemed to fancy that there would be no trouble at all about spinning along over the country, once he "got the hang of things."

"I'm bound to pull off some stunts while we're up here," he remarked, as he sat and looked at his prized possessions, now fastened with the straps to the toes of his shoes, leaving the heels free; "and I only hope the snow gets knee-deep by morning. I've read about how hunters up here in Canada chase the moose when a crust forms on the deep snow, and I want to try it for myself."

"That is reckoned the best time for hunting," Phil explained; "though it doesn't seem hardly fair to the caribou or the moose. You see, with their weight and their sharp hoofs they break through the crust at every jump, and flounder more or less in the drifts; while the hunter on his broad snow-shoes glides swiftly along, and can easily overtake the strongest of them."

"How about those moose yards I've read about?" asked Ethan, who though a descendant of a New England family knew much less about big-game hunting than did Phil.

"Oh! they are found in New Brunswick, and parts of Canada as well," the other explained. "When the snow gets very deep, so that the moose find it hard to move around in the woods, they make their way to some place previously selected, where they can feed on the tender shoots of certain trees. There they stay, trampling the snow down constantly, until the place looks like an enclosure surrounded by walls of snow."

"Then that's how it came to be called a moose yard, I suppose?" ventured Lub, who was listening to all of this talk, even though he did not profess to be very fond of hunting.

"Yes," Phil continued; "and there are some hunters so low down in the scale as real sportsmen that if they ran upon one of these yards they would take advantage of the opportunity to slaughter every one of the moose in it, no matter if they numbered ten or a dozen."

"But good gracious! isn't there a law limiting the number of moose any one person can shoot in a year?" asked Lub.

"Of course there is, and it's generally a single specimen, because moose are getting more and more scarce every season," said Phil; "but what does the game law signify to these hogs? So long as they can feel pretty sure of not being found out there's nothing too mean for them to do."

"What a shame they can't all be arrested, and sent up for a term of years," Lub remarked, indignantly.

"And don't think for a minute," Ethan broke in with, "that it's the guides who do things like that. They know better than to kill the goose that lays the golden egg for them. On the contrary, as a rule it is some reckless so-called sportsman who allows his primal passion to have full play when he finds himself up against such a golden opportunity. And I suppose he even makes his boasts of what great feats he performed when he finds himself back home with other fellows about the same build as himself."

The snow was by this time falling heavily. If it kept up at that rate, by morning it would certainly be measured by a dozen inches. X-Ray was so tickled he could hardly think of taking his snow-shoes off, but sat there a long time admiring the bent wood and stretched gut contrivances which men have used for so many years as a means for getting over the drifts of these cold countries.

"Looks like you meant to sit up all night, admiring yourself, X-Ray!" suggested Ethan finally, with a little touch of sarcasm in his voice.

"Better put a chain on him, and make sure he doesn't scoot out in the night!" Lub sang out.

"That word scoot makes me think of the motorboat we had down there on old Currituck Sound a while back," chuckled X-Ray, not at all bothered it seemed by these remarks on the part of his chums; "you remember it was called the Skoot, though for that matter it belied its name, for it never could go fast."

Soon afterward, however, X-Ray relieved Lub's anxious mind by removing the snow-shoes, and saying as he did so:

"Guess I can wait till to-morrow for my run; and, Phil, remember, you gave me your solemn promise to keep me company the first chance that came along?"

"We'll see," was all Phil would admit.

"Lucky we got our bully little shack all done before this started in, eh, boys?" remarked Ethan.

"It held off for us, which was a mighty fine thing for the weather to do," Lub told them, as he changed around in order to get his back warm, for he was now thinking of turning in.

They had arranged it so that the shack could be closed against the weather in time of stress. Phil made sure they had an abundance of fuel handy, for he said they would need it right along. The fire was to be kept up through the night; for a certain amount of heat might be expected to enter the lean-to through the opening where the canvas apron was drawn aside.

The fresh meat was hung from a limb, and high enough from the ground to prevent any wandering wolf from jumping up and carrying it off. Lub had been very solicitous about that part of the program, instructing the others to make sure by actual tests that it was a sufficient distance from the ground.

"Bear meat is too hard to get," he said, with considerable pride, "to want to feed it to the sneaking wolves."

Of course the others indulged in another pantomime laugh, as though they quite enjoyed hearing the peace-loving Lub talk in that strain. It did them no harm, and seemed to afford Lub more or less pleasure, so none of them attempted to shatter his dream of conquest by rude remarks.

Although X-Ray Tyson was the one most interested in the snowfall he never aroused himself enough at any time during the night to crawl out and take an observation as to the state of the weather.

Phil and Ethan looked after the fire; though on several occasions when one of them reentered the shack after performing this duty a sleepy voice would inquire after the weather conditions, and on hearing that the snow was still falling heavily X-Ray would grunt his usual phrase:

"That's hunky-dory; let her come!"

With the arrival of morning there could no longer be any doubt that winter had set in for good. A foot of snow on the level, with many drifts that were several times that deep, told how busy the old man plucking geese aloft had been while the Mountain Boys slept.

X-Ray was wild with delight.

"At last my day has come around!" he kept repeating over and over; "the day I've been waiting for so long. When shall we make a start, Phil?"

"Certainly not till after we've had a good hot breakfast, for one thing," asserted the other; "and if it keeps on falling like it does now nothing would tempt me to start out for a snow-shoe tramp."

"But it looks to me like the clouds were ready to break over there in the northwest," urged the eager one.

"Let her break, then," Phil told him; "time enough to talk about going when we see the sun peeping out. I understand it's no soft snap to get twisted up in this same Canadian bush, with a blizzard blowing the snow down, and the cold getting away below zero point."

"Whoo! excuse me if you please," spoke up Lub; "I'll take mine out alongside this cheery blaze. Somebody has got to eat the drumsticks, my mother always says; and even in camp there must be a cook."

"And a jolly good one we happen to have along with us!" remarked X-Ray, generously.

"No taffy, please," warned Lub. "I may take a notion to strike, one of these days, and then the rest of you would have to throw up heads or tails to see who takes my place."

"We hope that day will be a long way off," declared the wily Ethan, "because the chances are we'd have to come to eating that erbswurst just as it is, because no one could do justice to the culinary department after being spoiled the way we have."

Of course Lub was not so green as to think they meant all they said; yet at the same time it must have been pleasant for him to know his valiant efforts over the fire were appreciated by his chums. He worked harder than ever, and the satisfied smile that spread over his rosy face told that his thoughts were happy.

After all X-Ray was right about those clouds, although he did not claim to be a weather prophet, as he had once done. Even as they sat there and made away with the fine breakfast that had been prepared a bright ray of sunlight fell aslant the party; and looking out they could see that the snow had a dazzling appearance.

"Bully for that!" cried X-Ray; "if I didn't have my breakfast in my lap I'd feel like jumping up and dancing a hornpipe for joy. That means we'll soon be starting forth on our snow-shoes, eh, Phil?"

"I suppose you'll never give me a minute's peace until I do go out with you," the other declared, with a laugh; "though it's pretty hard work paddling around on snow-shoes when there isn't a trace of crust on top of the fall to hold you up. You see, every step you have to drag a shoe after you, and when the stuff is soft it means real work."

"Well, you never were known to go back on your word, rain or shine," said the other, in a satisfied sort of way, as though he did not mean to let it worry him in the least.

Half an hour later they were getting in readiness for the start.

"We'll carry our guns of course," said Phil, "for we might run across a caribou, and just now a little venison in camp wouldn't come in bad. And make sure to take plenty of ammunition along, for while we may not need it you never can tell. Likewise some matches besides your usual supply. I'll put up a snack for our lunch; and besides we can carry some of that pemmican from the six pound can. Nothing to equal it as a life-saver in a pinch."

"Whew! to hear you talk," said the astonished Lub, "one would think you really expected to get lost, and roam through the bush for days before you struck our own camp again; but of course you don't, Phil?"

"If I did think so I'd hesitate about going out," the other told him. "In doing what I am, Lub, I'm only taking out an insurance policy. No man expects a fire is really going to come and eat up his house; it's the last thing he looks for; and yet all the same he wants his mind to be at ease. If it should hit him he is in a condition to rebuild again. Well, chances are ten to one we'll bring this condensed food back with us; but in case we do need it we'll be mighty glad we have it along. And that's the right kind of policy to follow when you're off in the bush; for it is often the unexpected that happens."

Presently they had looked after every minute detail that could be thought of; and as X-Ray was very impatient to be off Phil did not have the heart to delay any longer.

"Here we go to hit the snow-shoe trail!" sang out the exultant X-Ray; and then he found it necessary to go through some violent contortions of the body in order to keep himself from tripping over his own feet, encumbered as they were with such unaccustomed appendages.

Phil had given him a staff, however, which he was expected to use in case of any need; and this prevented him from falling.

A minute later, and waving good-by to the others the two started forth.

CHAPTER VI – A QUARREL OVER THE GAME

"I'm getting to do first-rate at it, don't you think, Phil?" asked X-Ray, after they had been moving along for an hour and more.

"Yes, you seem to have mastered the trick all right," he was told, "though you did take a few headers when you grew too confident. Snow-shoes can only be successfully mastered through experience. They are clumsy things to a novice, and apt to play all sorts of sly tricks on him. I've seen a chap with both feet sticking up out of a drift; and unable to get out alone."

"Yes, I'd think they would act about the same as a life preserver fastened down around a fellow's knees. The very thing you are depending on to save you turns out your worst enemy when you treat it the wrong way. Now watch me make a little speed, Phil."

"Take care. Pride goes before a fall, they say. There, that's the time you did manage to tumble in good earnest."

"Help me up, that's a good fellow, Phil. I guess I'll feel my way after this. You may think you have mastered snow-shoes, but as you say they can spring a trick on you unawares. Your feet get twisted, and of course down you flop. But I'm satisfied with as far as I've gotten. The next thing is to learn to slide over a crust like the wind, climbing rises, and spinning down the other side like you were on skis. Say, it must be great sport; I hope it melts a little soon, and then freezes on top."

"Probably it will, now that you have expressed a wish that way," chuckled Phil, who was really having more or less fun observing the actions of the new beginner.

A short time later and Phil uttered an exclamation.

"What have you struck now?" asked X-Ray, eagerly.

Phil pointed to the snow close by.

"Some animal has gone along here, sure enough!" said X-Ray, bending over to examine the marks more closely. "A moose most likely, eh, Phil?"

"No, it was a caribou," the other assured him.

"A horse of another color, then; but it means game, all the same, Phil?"

"Yes, caribou are classed in that list, and make pretty good eating, too," the other explained.

"Of course we might take a little turn after the old chap, just to give me my first snow-shoe hunt; say yes, Phil."

"There's no reason that I can see why we shouldn't, though we don't want to get too far away from camp, because it's heavy work dragging a pair of shoes after you, once you begin to feel tired."

"We can stop whenever you think it's best," promised X-Ray.

Accordingly they began to follow the trail. It was so easy any novice could have done it; and yet there was a certain thrilling sensation about the whole matter that gave the new beginner much pleasure.

He had so often pictured himself in some such scene as this that the reality afforded him more genuine delight than words could describe.

Phil allowed him to take the lead, thinking that would satisfy X-Ray; who while not so fond of hunting as Ethan, at the same time was able to enjoy it to a certain extent.

With the trees all heavily laden with snow, some of the birches and pines bent almost double under the burden, it was a beautiful scene by which the two boys found themselves surrounded. Phil admired everything as he went along. X-Ray seemed to be thinking only of the chance they might have to come up with the caribou, and wondering if they would have the good luck to bring it down in case they did sight it.

He had never seen a caribou in his life, though he knew they were a species of deer inhabiting the barrens of New Brunswick and Canada, where they are often run across in herds of hundreds.

The snow was deep enough to give considerable trouble to the animal they were following, though it seemed that he kept persistently on. He was possibly heading for a certain rendezvous where he knew he would find others of his kind assembled, to pass the severe weather in company, as a protection against roving wolves that would soon bring a straggler down, yet dare not attack a herd.

X-Ray was more or less excited. Every little while he would in a whisper ask his companion what he thought about it, and if they were drawing up on the caribou.

"Seems to me the trail is getting a heap fresher," X-Ray suggested; though truth to tell that was put forward as a "feeler" to draw out an opinion from Phil, and not because he knew much about the tracks.

"Yes, it is getting fresher all the time," admitted Phil; "which shows that we are making much better time than the caribou. But it remains to be seen whether he can put on a burst of speed when he sights us that will leave us far in the lurch. He may be taking it easy along here."

"And what if he does flicker away and out of sight before we can drop him, Phil; do we keep up the good work, or drop out?"

"If he once gets going good and hard," Phil declared, "we might as well say good-day to him, and head back toward the camp."

"The camp! Well, if you asked me now, I couldn't tell you which way we'd have to go to get there; but of course you know, Phil? You always were a great hand to keep tabs of things."

"Yes, I've been watching our course all the while," Phil told him, confidently.

"And whereabouts would you say the camp lay from here, then?" asked X-Ray.

Without the slightest hesitation Phil pointed straight into the southeast.

"If you started off and kept a bee-line that way I believe you'd come within pistol-shot of our shack," he affirmed. "When you struck the shore of the lake it would be easy to locate the camp by the smoke rising, if not from other landmarks that every wise hunter would have jotted down in his memory."

X-Ray did not continue the low conversation immediately; he was trying to remember if there was any such landmark that he might have noticed close to the camp, and on the ice-bound shore of the lake.

"Oh! yes, there was the odd-shaped tree that looked like an old man on his knees and saying his prayers!" he broke out with, a look of satisfaction crossing his face at being able to recollect; "that was near by, and I think I would know it from across the lake if I happened to strike in there."

"I'm glad you remembered," said Phil; "but suppose we stop whispering now."

"Oh, my, do you expect we're as close to him as all that, Phil?" demanded X-Ray, beginning to finger at the lock of his gun, in order to make sure it was in readiness for quick use in an emergency.

"He passed along here just a bit ago, for a fact," Phil told him.

They continued to push on, with that trail always before them, though sometimes they turned aside on account of the barrier presented by a growth of bushes, through which the caribou had gone.

Phil had now come up alongside his companion, and noticing this X-Ray believed things must be quickly getting to a stage when something was liable to happen. He was expecting to see the caribou ahead of them at some little distance, and paid but small attention to points close at hand.

When without the least warning there was a sudden rattling sound heard, and a large brown animal was seen departing with great leaps, X-Ray gave utterance to a gasp of disappointment.

Even as the two young hunters threw their guns to their shoulders the fleeting caribou suddenly shifted its course, and turning abruptly to the right, sped on. It now presented a splendid mark, and the two shots rang out almost as one.

A remarkable thing happened just then. With the crash of their rifles the animal was seen to leap high in the air, just as deer often will when stricken in full flight. And to the astonishment of the boys another report sounded from the other side of the caribou!

"He's down, Phil!" shrilled X-Ray, trembling with the excitement.

"Yes, come on!" replied the other, immediately starting forward as fast as he could go on his snow-shoes.

"But, Phil, wasn't that another shot we heard?" expostulated X-Ray Tyson, as he did his level best to keep close to the heels of his chum.

"Yes, it was a gunshot," snapped Phil, who seemed to be laboring under some sort of emotion, though X-Ray could not say what its character might be.

They could see where the caribou had struck when he fell. His antlered head was resting on the snow, showing that he had fallen with that last leap, with his legs under him.

Phil saw a figure advancing from the opposite quarter, and also on snow-shoes. He was pleased to note there was only one, for he anticipated that there was likely to be trouble of some sort around that locality before long.

"There the other hunter comes, Phil!" said X-Ray, wanting to be sure that his chum was made aware of the important fact.

"All right, but we're going to get up before he does," was all Phil replied.

The first thing he did on reaching the spot where the stricken caribou lay was to bend down and closely examine the right side. As said before the animal lay just as it had fallen, so that both haunches were in plain view, did any one take the trouble to step around.

Phil was gratified with what he saw in that hasty survey; but nevertheless he immediately leaned over to ascertain the condition of the animal's left side. By that time X-Ray had come up, and the stranger sportsman was also close at hand.

Up to that moment Phil had not taken the pains to give the other a look; but as he had found out all he wanted concerning the state of affairs in connection with the game, he now turned his attention on the advancing man.

He was a rather stout and exceedingly peppery looking individual, who was rather out of breath, and puffing from his exertions. His florid face did not impress Phil favorably at all; it seemed to sense the bully, and the overbearing man of millions, accustomed to lording it over others.

There was no question at all in Phil's mind but that this man was a member of the other party he had been told was in camp in that vicinity. He might have even thought him to be a beef-eating Englishman only that his information had been to the effect that they were all Americans from below the border.

"I don't like his looks!" muttered X-Ray.

"No more do I," added Phil, under his breath, for the stranger sportsman was getting close up by then, and might hear if words were spoken in an ordinary tone. "But the game is ours without a question, and we're going to have what we want to carry off, make up your mind to that."

"Bully!" muttered X-Ray, who was inclined to be pugnacious on occasion; and at any rate never disposed to allow himself to be "used as a door mat, for some other person to wipe his feet on," as he used to put it.

Perhaps Phil meant something when he calmly placed his foot on the fallen game. It was a significant move, at any rate, and could hardly be mistaken. It struck X-Ray as peculiarly defiant, and he felt like chuckling as he watched to see what that red-faced individual did when he arrived on the scene of action.

If anything his face took on a deeper tint until it looked almost purple. When he saw that he had only two boys to contend with the other hunter must have believed he could frighten them with his looks, for he scowled like a pirate.

Somehow neither of the Mountain Boys drew back and began to apologize for daring to rob him of any of the free air. And no sooner had he arrived than the domineering tactics, with which perhaps he had pushed himself through business so as to accumulate his million, began to make themselves manifest.

"Here, what are you doing with your foot on my caribou, I'd like to know?" was what he jerked out, being still short of breath.

"Excuse me, sir, but you'll have to explain what you mean," said Phil, coolly. "I am not aware of taking any such liberties with your caribou. If it happens that you are referring to this animal here, you've made a big mistake, that's all. It is our game; we saw it first, shot it first, and got here first. So you'll have to go to court and put in a claim. Possession in this case is nine points of the law!"

The man stared at the speaker. He evidently had seldom been spoken to in that manner before, certainly never by a mere boy. And yet something in Phil's face must have impressed him as worth observing. He saw that those eyes were fastened on him with a steady and keen look that did not falter under his scowl, or his muttering.

"I tell you it is my caribou, for I shot it," he proceeded to affirm, embellishing his assertion with certain strong words which he doubtless expected might make the boys hesitate before they went any further and incurred his ill-will. "I was just creeping up within easy gunshot when you came along and scared the beast. I claim it as my prize."

"And we have been trailing the same caribou for at least two hours," said X-Ray under the impression that since he was a party to the dispute he should at least be allowed to get a few words in.

"The matter is easily settled," said Phil, quietly.

"I am glad to see that you mean to act sensibly; for since you came up after I had started to stalk the caribou it put you in the wrong," the other said, as if rather relieved in his mind at the turn affairs had taken.

"Don't mistake me, sir," continued Phil; "what I meant was that we can easily prove which has the right to the game. There's a way to settle that question that neither of us can rightly deny. If you look over here at this side of the caribou, which was the side toward us, you remember, you will find that two bullets entered his body, one directly in the region of his heart. That shot killed the animal instantly. He could only make one jump, and then collapsed as you see him."

"Humph!" grunted the stout red-faced sportsman, with one of his ugly frowns; "and I suppose then you'll make out that I missed him entirely?"

"I'm not making out anything, sir, for you can see from the red mark just where your lead cut a little section from his hind leg. I'm sure I heard it sing past me and hardly ten feet away. That hurt would never have crippled a strong beast like a young bull caribou. You would never have had the least chance to lay claim to any of the meat if you had depended on your shot. But we're not greedy, sir; and if you care to forget this little unpleasantness we'll gladly call it our combined trophy of the chase, and divide the meat with you!"

It was a generous offer, and did the boy credit; but apparently the quarrelsome sportsman with the purple face felt himself insulted by being patronized by a couple of boys, for he ground his teeth together, and looked daggers at Phil.

CHAPTER VII — NOT TO BE BLUFFED

"I mean to have all, or none!" and as he said these words the red-faced hunter glowered at Phil as though he felt like eating him, X-Ray afterwards declared.

"Suit yourself, sir," remarked the boy, coolly drawing out his hunting knife.

The man looked a little startled; perhaps he thought Phil intended to attack him.

"Be careful what you mean to do, boy!" he stammered, some of the color leaving his fade; but he saw that X-Ray stood there with his gun under his arm, and finger playing with the lock, so he dared not try to elevate his own weapon in order to threaten Phil.

"I expect to cut this caribou up," said Phil, firmly. "Half of it is as much as we care to tote back to our camp with us. I shall leave the balance here. You can take it or leave it, as you choose, sir. It matters nothing to us."

He turned and said something in so low a tone to X-Ray that the sportsman could not catch its import. Since the other boy immediately drew back the hammer of his repeating rifle, and swung the weapon slightly around until it was pointing directly at the man he could easily guess what Phil had told his chum.

"Perhaps you do not know who I am," blustered the owner of the red face.

"Well, you haven't taken the trouble to introduce yourself yet, I believe, sir," Phil told him.

"My name is James Bodman, and I am interested in American railways!"

It was amusing to see the way the stout party drew himself up proudly as he said this. Of course Phil knew instantly that he was face to face with one of the best known millionaire railroad owners in the whole United States; and he also remembered reading that the same James Bodman was noted as a domineering financial despot.

Phil did not flinch. He gave no sign of being greatly impressed by the importance of the other's position in the world of finance. Instead he merely flirted his hand around to indicate his chum, and remarked with the greatest indifference possible:

"Oh! is that so? Well, let me introduce my friend, Raymond Tyson, Mr. Bodman. As for myself I'm Phil Bradley."

That was all Phil said.

He immediately started work on the fallen caribou, with an air of business that could not brook delay. There were some miles of snowy bush to be traversed before he and his comrade could expect to reach their camp, and he did not wish to be detained any more than was absolutely necessary.

Meanwhile X-Ray was having considerable fun in watching the expressions that chased each other across the florid countenance of the stout hunter. Mr. Bodman apparently found himself taken aback by the indifferent manner in which the news of his identity was received. He had possibly expected the boys to be dazed, and perhaps hasten to beg his august pardon.

"Huh! you'll be sorry for this, let me tell you!" he finally burst out with.

"So?" Phil simply said, as he continued with deft strokes to hack away at the part of the dead caribou's carcass he meant to carry off with him.

Unable to stay there and be defied so boldly, the sportsman turned his back on his tormentors. He looked as though he might be close on having a fit of some kind the last they saw of him.

Once he turned and shook his fist in their direction. X-Ray half raised his gun, as though to let him understand two could play at that game if he dreamed of firing at them; but apparently Mr. Bodman had no intention of risking a shot, for he moved away clumsily on his snow-shoes, with which he was no adept, it appeared.

X-Ray chuckled as though tremendously amused.

"Just hear him growling like a bear with a sore head, will you, Phil? My stars! but he does hate a fellow who has the gall to sass him to his face. I guess he's so swelled up with a sense of his importance, that he expects everybody to fall to trembling when he says so high and mighty like: 'I am James Bodman, huh!'"

"I feel that I did the right thing, X-Ray," said Phil, working away industriously.

"You were more than generous to offer him half, when he didn't deserve a pound of this meat," said the other, scornfully. "What if he did draw blood, that wound wouldn't have feazed the caribou even a little bit. But it seems that Mr. Bodman's policy has been rule or ruin all his life, and he can't get away from it. In plain language I'd call him the Great American Hog."

"I'd hate to have any dealings with that sort of a man," Phil continued. "He's the kind that always wants the best, and others can take the leavings."

"That's how he got his millions, I reckon," X-Ray suggested. "Seems that there's a glut in the market of hard cases up here in this Canadian bush while we're on our little hunt, what with this bully, and that other one to boot."

"Meaning Anson Baylay, the poacher, and all-round terror of the backwoods, eh, X-Ray?"

"Say, I'd give something to see those two run up against each other, and have it out. The free show would beat the old one you hear about, when

"'There once were two cats in Kilkenny,

And each thought there was one cat too many.

So they quarreled and fit; and they gouged and they bit,

Till save the tips of their nails and the ends of their tails,

There was naught left of the two cats of Kilkenny.'"

"It looks to me as if this Mr. Bodman might be a bad hater," mused Phil; "and all I hope is he doesn't get a chance to give us trouble while we're up here."

"Why, how could he do that, Phil; the woods are free to every one; and I'm sure we paid for our hunting licenses as he did, if he is worth his millions. In what way could he injure us?"

"Mind, I don't say he will try to do anything," urged Phil. "Fact is, I hope on second thought the man may come to the conclusion he made a fool of himself. Perhaps he'll hide until we go away, and then return to get his share of the meat. He may even keep it secret that he met his match in two American boys. That would end the matter, so far as we are concerned."

"I suppose he's got a pretty hard crowd over with him in his camp; that lumber-jack gave us to understand as much. They might take a notion to make it unpleasant for us up here, so we'd want to clear out. But they'd better go slow. The Mountain Boys can stand up for their rights."

"Let's forget all about the unpleasant experience, and talk of other things," was Phil's wise suggestion.

Later on, when he had secured all the meat they would care to carry, at least a fair half of the carcass remained untouched.

"If he cares to come back and cut it up he's welcome," said Phil, as they prepared to leave the scene of the killing; "if not, I warrant you there will be only clean-picked bones here by to-morrow morning."

"Yes, with so many hungry wolves hanging around," added X-Ray; "if they're all like that one we bagged at our camp they could clean up a mess like this in half a jiffy."

Nothing occurred on the way home, and in good time the two weary snow-shoe trampers came in sight of the lake and the camp.

When it was learned that they had been successful in their search for a caribou the other two expressed considerable delight; Lub because it would be a new kind of food for them to experiment on, and Ethan regarding the exploit with the interest of a born hunter.

"And, Phil?" the latter immediately broke out with, "to-morrow I hope you'll take another little trip with me. I kind of think I know where we can get a moose; and you've been saying you want to shoot one in the snow forest with your camera."

"How is that?" demanded Phil, naturally interested at once.

"Why, I took a little turn around this afternoon, just to exercise my pins, and practice with my show-shoes, because I'm not as clever at it as you. And I just had a glimpse of a big moose scooting off through the brush."

"Did you fire at the beast?" asked Phil; "because if you wounded him the chances are he'd keep on going as long as he could move his hoofs, and we'd never get a sight of him again."

"Why, no, I hope I'm too good a sportsman to shoot recklessly when there isn't one chance in a hundred of my bringing the game down," said Ethan a little indignantly. "I want to be fairly sure when I throw lead; I don't believe in giving any animal unnecessary pain."

"Excuse me, Ethan, I ought to have known you better than to ask that. And if the day is anyway decent I'll promise to take a wide turn with you."

"Thank you, Phil, for saying that; and I hope on my part we get close enough up for you to snap off the old bull moose before we drop him."

"Did you see that it was a bull?" asked the other, curiously.

"Well, no, I didn't for a fact," replied Ethan; "I just caught sight of the big beast; then the brush closed behind him, and left me staring, with my gun half way up to my shoulder. But it was a good-sized one, let me tell you, even making allowances for any little excitement on my part."

The caribou had chanced to be a young one, which Phil considered fortunate indeed. Lub did his very best at cooking the steaks cut from the joint, but for all that none of the boys seemed to be wildly pleased with the meat. The fact probably was they had too many good things along with them; had their larder been empty, and their stomachs craving food, that meal would have been a real hunters' feast without a doubt.

"I think we're doing remarkably well, so far," Lub was saying, after they were through with supper, and sat around in lazy attitudes, enjoying the sparkle and glow of the comfortable fire; "what with getting a real savage wolf, a walking bear, and now a caribou, the last a species of deer which none of us have ever seen before."

"Yes, all we need now to complete the string of big game to be found up here is a moose, together with a lynx that has tassels on its ears," laughed Ethan; "and to-morrow may bring that list down to the cat tribe, if Phil and myself have any luck on our tramp."

"I'm wondering how I can set my usual flashlight trap up here of nights, so as to get a few pictures of Canadian wild animals in their native haunts," Phil remarked. "If any of you happen to glimpse the tracks of a fox, or a mink, or any sort of little beast, be sure and let me know. I want to follow the trail up and learn where he has his haunt, so I can lay for him."

"How about the beaver houses Mr. McNab told us we might find up that stream, unless some sportsmen or fur-gatherers have cleaned the colony out?" Ethan asked.

"I was thinking of that," replied Phil, "and there may be a chance for us to hit that same stream on our way to-morrow. So I think I'll carry my camera along, and be ready."

"I've seen their houses behind a dam they'd made," remarked Ethan; "but it was in the early fall. A place like that must look picturesque when the snow is everywhere around."

"I hope we can find the colony pond, and that the hard working beaver haven't been cleaned out," Phil continued; after which the conversation drifted into other channels, though Ethan would not be apt to forget when the morrow came, for he was always a great hand to recollect things.

The night had closed in as cold as ever, and it was easy to be seen that winter was getting a good firm grip up here in the far northern wilderness of Canada, and in the famous Saguenay River region.

With all the comforts they had at hand the boys did not dream of complaining; in fact they were thoroughly enjoying every minute of their stay. Even X-Ray, who a year back had been rather inclined to seem sickly, was showing a remarkable improvement in his physique, partly due no doubt to these days and nights, spent in the open air, when on excursions with his three chums.

Long they sat there before the cheery camp fire, laughing, singing some of their school songs, telling stories, and having the time of their lives, as Lub declared.

The stout chum insisted on having the skin of "his" bear close to him most of the time, and he was very fond of running his hand down the long shaggy hair in a caressing way. He hoped he would be able to impress those fellows at home in Brewster with the wonderful value of being smart enough to lure a bear within gunshot of his comrades. And surely none of them would be so mean as to sneer at his claim to the quarry on that score.

At any rate trials so far in the future could not give happy-go-lucky Lub any harassing care. He was in fine spirits on this particular night, and kept the others in roars of laughter with his comical sayings, and his songs.

Later on they sought their blankets. The program of the previous night was duplicated, and the fire kept burning through the long hours when darkness held sway over the primeval wilderness.

Morning showed no important change in the weather conditions, for which Ethan at least was glad. X-Ray grumbled a little, because he had hoped a short thaw might set in, so they could have a glaze of thin ice on top of that deep blanket of snow, for he wanted now to try his hand at gliding swiftly over the levels, climbing ascents after a fashion, and spinning down the slopes beyond like the wind.

Ethan was ready soon after breakfast, and Phil did not detain him long, waiting only to make sure that as on the previous day they carried such things along with them as would come in handy in case they found themselves detained longer than they figured on.

Lub and X-Ray gave them a parting cheer.

"Make it moose for supper to-night, fellows!" called the latter.

"Variety is the spice of life, you know!" Lub told them; "and since I've got my hand in so well at cooking, nothing scares me these days. Why, I'd as soon try a steak of elephant meat, a piece of a giraffe, or perhaps a monkey roast. So-long, boys, and good-luck to you all!"

CHAPTER VIII — AGAIN ON THE TRAIL

"Here's about where I stood when I heard something rushing off, and looked just in time to get a peek at the moose."

As he said this Ethan pointed down to where the marks of his snow-shoes could be plainly seen.

"Now lead me to where you saw the moose, which I take it must have been over there in that direction," remarked Phil.

"As sure as you live," declared the other; "and I guess you knew that from the way my tracks set, eh, Phil?"

"Just what I did look at the first thing," confessed the other.

Presently they were bending over the trail in the deep snow which showed where the alarmed moose had gone plunging off.

"It's a moose, all right," Phil admitted, without much delay.

"Can you tell if it was a bull?" asked the other.

"Well, not from the tracks. Did you happen to notice any horns on the beast?" was what Phil inquired.

"I can't just say I did; but then it all happened so quick I couldn't be dead sure either way. It's a good-sized critter anyway, I think, Phil."

"Yes, no doubt about that, Ethan. But let's get started on the trail."

That pleased Ethan, for he was full of eagerness. The love for hunting ran full and strong in his veins. Phil used to be built in the same way, but since discovering the peculiar fascination of hunting with a flashlight camera he seemed to be losing much of his former liking for killing game. He would much rather spend his time playing his skill and brains against the natural caution of the wearers of fur, in endeavoring to photograph them in their native haunts.

For a while they continued to move along. Sometimes they could make pretty good speed, where the going was easy; and then again it became necessary to push through thickets where the branches were so thick as to hold them up.

"Have you any idea yet whether it's a bull or a cow?" asked Ethan, after they must have been going fully two hours.

"Not absolutely," returned Phil; "but I've got an idea we're going to find it the latter."

"Tell me what you base your judgment on, please, Phil."

"I may be all wrong at that," replied the other, who never set himself up as infallible. "There have been a few places where the chase led us through thick woods, with the lower limbs of the trees hanging down under their snow burden just so far. If the moose had big horns, which would be the case in a bull, no matter how far back on his shoulders he laid them they would be apt to break some of the twigs loose above, and we'd have seen them lying on the snow."

"Then I take it from what you say there were none of these signs, eh, Phil?"

"Not that I could see, and I looked carefully, not once but several times. I'm afraid, Ethan, your moose is going to turn out a big cow after all."

"And we promised ourselves we wouldn't shoot a cow moose even if we had to go without such big game, didn't we, Phil?"

"That's where I have the bulge on you, Ethan," laughed the other.

"As how?" demanded the eager hunter; "you sure subscribed to that rule with the rest of us, Phil."

"Yes, but only so far as my gun went," he was told; "I can shoot that cow with my camera, and never injure a hair of her hide, you see."

At that Ethan shrugged his shoulders, and made a grimace.

"Yes, that's a fact, you have got the jump on us, Phil. But I suppose, then, we can keep on the move, and take our chance of catching up with the cow, so as to let you get in a snap-shot of the same?"

"We'll keep going up, to a certain limit," figured Phil; "I wouldn't care to tramp beyond that. We'd want to be able to make the home camp by night, you know."

"As for that," said Ethan, indifferently, "what should we worry about even if we had to stay out a night? Fact is, I'd rather enjoy the experience in your company. So don't count me in when you're figuring things, Phil. I c'n take pot-luck any old time."

As on the previous day Phil could readily tell that they were gaining on the animal they followed. He had shown Ethan where the moose spent the previous night and it seemed as though the animal could not have been very greatly alarmed by seeing the young hunter, for it had not gone more than two miles after that before stopping to browse upon some tender branches of a certain tree, and stop until another day dawned.

The trail did not always keep on in a direct line, but there was more or less of a zigzag movement about it. From this Phil drew the conclusion that the moose must be scouring the bush in hopes of meeting up with others of its kind, so as to keep company with them for the balance of the long winter.

It began to get along toward high noon.

Ethan felt hungry, since they had been on the tramp a long while now. Still he did not dream of stopping to build a fire, and waste time with such foolishness, thus losing most of the advantage they had gained.

"We can chew at something as we keep right along, eh, Phil?" he remarked, after mentioning the subject of lunch.

"Yes, unless we come up with our game before the sun is at the zenith," the other replied. "Of course, after we've met the moose we needn't be in such a hurry, and an hour's rest would make both of us feel a heap better for the return journey."

Apparently Ethan was quite content to let it go at that, for he did not mention the subject again.

A short time afterward Phil whispered that the trail was so fresh he would not be surprised if they came in sight of the moose at any moment. He had slung his gun to his back and held his camera ready for instant use in case the chance came.

Of course they could never have come so close to the animal had the wind been blowing from them toward the moose; but the animal followed the habit of most of the deer tribe in advancing into the wind, so as to be able to detect any danger ahead.

Then all at once Ethan gave a low cry.

"Look, Phil!"

There was a snap, and Phil had secured a picture of a big animal not unlike a hornless domestic cow standing there staring at them. He even had time to roll the film and get his camera in condition for business again before, with a sudden plunge the unwieldy beast went off through the drifts.

"Got two beauty shots at her, didn't you?" queried Ethan; "oh! what a dandy chance for me to pull trigger, if it had only been a big bull with massive horns. But I'm glad for your sake there was so fine a picture. It ought to make a dandy showing, with the snow woods for a background, and those dark firs on the right."

Of course now that the excitement was all over the boys began to feel somewhat tired after such tedious walking with the clumsy snow-shoes; so when Phil suggested that they find a good place, make a cheerful fire, and sit around in comfort while they ate their lunch, there was no objection from his companion.

A fire is certainly the hunter's best friend, in winter time at least. Without it how gloomy and cheerless would his surroundings appear, and what physical discomfort must he endure?

The two boys sat there for more than an hour, a friendly log serving them for a seat.

There was plenty of fuel to be had for the gathering; indeed, the site had been selected on that very account.

"I'm trying to make out just which way we ought to go so as to strike that little stream," Phil was saying, when the other asked what he was doing with a pencil and paper.

"Oh! you mean the one McNab called Cranberry Creek, and that has the beaver colony on it, somewhere like five miles from our lake; is that it, Phil?"

"Yes, and this is how I figure it," continued the other, showing what he had done in drawing a rough map on the paper. "Here is the camp on the lake; this is the way we got to where we are sitting now, having headed pretty generally into the north. This is the way the creek runs, so if we start from here and keep bending a little to the west we're likely to strike the stream."

"Looks good to me, Phil."

"Then let's call that our program," Phil wound up with saying.

"According to the way you figure how long a distance would you think we'd have to cover before we got to the creek?" asked Ethan.

"Oh! anywhere between half a mile, and three times as far," the other told him.

"And after we reach the frozen creek," continued Ethan, "all we have to do is to follow it down to the lake, hoping to run across the beaver village on the way."

"Just so, and since we've rested and feel in good trim again, suppose we make a start right away?"

Ethan had no objections. He liked to be on the move, and besides, there may have been a lingering hope still lodged in his mind that they might happen to come upon a noble bull moose before the tramp was over. If there was one of those animals wandering around that region why not others?

So as he strode along Ethan was careful to keep in condition for business. And if by good luck they did happen on game he meant to do his type of shooting even as Phil pressed the button and featured the moose for admiring eyes at home to see.

They were heading pretty generally into the west, though it was Phil's idea to swing around gradually, and begin to aim more for the lake. Ethan left all that to his chum. He never boasted of his ability to keep track of localities; in fact, on numerous occasions Ethan had lost himself. It was a weakness, he admitted it, and one so ambitious a hunter ought to be ashamed of; but somehow Ethan rather enjoyed the sensation of finding himself suddenly thrown on his own resources, and being compelled to find his way out of a labyrinth.

"I always did like to solve any old puzzle when I was a little kid," he used to say when Phil took him to task for his lack of forethought in this particular, "and when you wake up to the knowledge that you're really and truly without your bearings, seems like you had a new and intricate riddle to guess. And I haven't starved to death yet, you notice. Guess I'll always be able to smell my way home, one way or another."

At the same time Ethan frankly confessed that his way was not the right one, and he did not advise any one else to copy after him. They might not enjoy the sensation like he did; or have that faculty for "smelling" home, the instinct that causes a bee to start on a straight line for the hive after loading itself up with nectar from the blossoms, even when a mile distant from home.

The cold seemed to be getting worse, if anything, and Ethan predicted that they would have a bitter night of it.

"But then what do we care?" he added, with a laugh; "with plenty of good grub, a warm fire under a snug shelter, and blankets to wrap around us, we can afford to snap our fingers at the cold weather clerk. Let him order out one of those Canada blizzards we've heard so much about, if he wants to give the Mountain Boys a run for their money."

"We must have covered a whole mile after leaving the place where we sat on that log and ate our lunch," remarked Phil.

"And no creek yet, as far as I've seen, Phil!"

"Nothing doing," admitted the other; "so I think we'd better begin to swing around a little more to the southwest from now on."

"You'll try another half mile, you said, didn't you?" asked Ethan.

"That will be all I care to risk. If the old creek hasn't cropped up by then we might as well give it up for to-day. Another time I'll start up from where it flows into the lake."

"That would be the better way, Phil; you'd make sure then of finding the beaver colony, if it was still there. As we're going we may even strike the creek below the dam, and have all our extra walk for nothing."

The woods seemed very still. Even the crows had gone somewhere for the day to find their rations. Early in the morning the boys had seen flocks flying in a certain quarter, and Phil had given it as his opinion they were heading toward a large lake that would not be frozen up so early in the winter, and along the shores of which doubtless crows could pick up plenty of food.

"Looks like I wasn't going to be treated to that shot at a moose to-day, at any rate," half grumbled Ethan, who had been considerably disappointed because the animal they had tracked so persistently had failed to turn out to be a bull with towering horns, and a fit subject for his skill with the rifle.

"Other days coming," Phil told him, consolingly; "and we've had a fine tramp on our snow-shoes to boast of, even if I hadn't secured the snapshots I did."

"Excuse me for speaking in the way I did, Phil; I forgot myself that time. It's all in a day's work, I guess. And I want you to understand that it's a treat for me just to get out in the woods along with you."

"I thought I heard something just then," said Phil, quickly, swinging his camera around so as to be ready; while Ethan drew back the hammer of his rifle once more, his eyes sparkling with renewed anticipation.

"Yes, I can get it, too, Phil," he whispered; "it sounds as if it might be over yonder in that thick patch of trees. Move a little to the left, so we can have a clear field in case it rushes out. Now let's advance slowly."

They kept on going ahead, and nothing burst into view. Still that queer sound came to their ears. It was not unlike a sob, Ethan thought; though he immediately took himself to task for imagining such a silly thing.

Picking up a stick he gave it a toss into the thicket. The sound stopped, it was true, but not a thing appeared.

Then a minute later and they heard it again. The two boys turned wondering eyes on each other.

"What in the dickens can it be?" whispered Ethan, in a puzzled way.

"I give it up; let's push in and see. Be ready, if it's a cat, which is the only thing I can think of," said Phil.

With that they started ahead again, and gradually working into the thicket soon found themselves staring at a sight calculated to amaze them.

CHAPTER IX—THE WAIF OF THE SNOW FOREST

Ethan winked several times as though he could hardly believe his eyes, and little wonder; for there, half lying in the snow was a child, a sturdy looking little chap not over five years of age possibly, and uttering sounds that the boys now realized were pitiful moans.

Apparently the little fellow had actually tried to light a fire, for there were a few sticks gathered, and half burned matches that had been struck in the useless endeavor to ignite the wood, lay scattered on the surface of the snow.

"Look at the little make-believe popgun, Phil," said Ethan, in a quivering voice; "honest to goodness, I believe he's started out to hunt game just as his daddy is in the habit of doing, and got lost. But, Phil, he must be nearly frozen. Let's get a fire going and thaw him out in a hurry!"

Phil had already leaped forward. Forgotten was his camera at that moment, because his generous warm boyish heart was throbbing with sympathy for the poor little chap lying there.

"How about it?" asked Ethan, hovering close by while the other hurriedly examined the boy, who lay there with his eyes half open, seeing them, yet not appearing to notice what they were doing, with only that doleful little cry falling from his blue lips.

"No, he's not frozen yet, I believe," asserted Phil; "but another hour would have done the business for him. I reckon he knew how to keep his arms going until he got tuckered out. Get a fire started, Ethan."

That was all the other was waiting to hear, and in all probability Ethan Allen excelled all his previous records for a quick blaze; because he worked with might and main.

Meanwhile Phil was rubbing the hands and limbs of the child, astonished beyond measure at having run across such a little fellow there in the midst of that Canadian wilderness.

"Here you are, Phil; fetch him up close to it!" called out the other boy, as he judiciously added further pieces of wood to the blaze he had contrived to start.

Neither of them could solve the problem as to where the little fellow had come from.

"He must have rained down," said Ethan; "or else he's been with that other party of sportsmen, and slipped away from their camp, bent on having a regular moose hunt of his own. Look at this popgun, will you; it's one of the kind that has a spring in it, and shoots B. B. shot. I've owned the same kind myself years ago. But what do you think, Phil?"

"I'm all up in the air," replied the other, candidly. "If he came from that other camp he couldn't be connected with any of those rich sportsmen, for you can see his clothes are those of poverty, though warm enough. He must belong to some Canadian backwoods family. It might be they've got a man and wife cooking for them in their camp, or the man as a guide and the woman to get the meals. And the child could belong to them, it might turn out."

"Didn't Mr. McNab tell us that terror of the pines, Anson Baylay, had several kids at his home, as well as a wife, a small woman who knew how to manage the big giant?" inquired Ethan.

"That's a fact!" declared Phil, looking again at the small boy; "I wonder now if this could be one of his brood? But when he gets so he can talk perhaps we'll be able to find out all about him."

"What's the program?" demanded Ethan; "we don't want to stay here, do we, hoping some one may come in search of the poor kid?"

"No, our best plan is get him to camp with all speed. He may not be as well off as I've hoped is the case. And with a night ahead of us, a shelter, with food and a fire will be good for all of us. Fact is, there's a change coming on; the sun has gone behind the clouds, and it wouldn't surprise me if we had one of those blizzards you're so fond of talking about."

"Well, for myself I wouldn't mind," said Ethan, loftily; "but it would be pretty tough on the little chap if we got caught in a howling storm, with the mercury going away down below zero. I'll take my turn carrying him, Phil, remember."

"We'll have to change about, because he's going to be no light load," Phil admitted; "I wish the boy would come to himself; he might tell us something that'd put us on the right track. But we're not going to wait for that."

With these words he gathered the little fellow up in his arms and started. Ethan on his part took charge of the guns, as well as the camera; and in this manner they headed in what Phil believed to be a bee-line for the camp.

It would have been no small task carrying the boy for any distance, even under ordinary conditions; and the fact of their being on snow-shoes made it all the more difficult.

Still, both of them were stalwart fellows, and able to do considerable along the line of carrying burdens. Their outdoor life had given them more strength than most boys of their age possessed.

Phil kept it up for quite a time.

"Better change off with me, now," Ethan hinted, for the fifth time.

"All right, then, Ethan; just lay those things down where I can get them, and I'll give you the boy. He's some heft, believe me, and a pretty chubby lad for his age, which I shouldn't take to be more than five, or six at the most."

"But isn't it queer he hasn't come to, and asked us who we are, and where we're taking him?" remarked the second boy, as he took the object of their solicitude into his arms.

"He'll come out of it all right later on, I feel pretty sure," Phil observed, as he loaded himself with the guns and camera, after which he started ahead of his companion so as to break the way.

"There's a dash of color beginning to show in his cheeks, I do believe!" called out Ethan, presently.

Later on he had to hand his burden over to the other; and this sort of thing continued many times, until all of two hours had gone.

Both boys were growing very tired after their long tramp, and now with carrying their human burden, too. But Phil buoyed up the spirits of his chum by saying that they were close on the camp.

"I can see where the lake lies over yonder," he remarked, when they chanced to be on a rise that gave them a chance to see around more or less; "and away over in that direction there's a black smoke rising that must come from the camp of that other party with James Bodman."

"But that isn't where we've just come from, Phil?" observed Ethan, shrewdly.

"Far away from it, to tell the truth, and I see what you mean, Ethan. It doesn't look as if this chap could ever have wandered away from that camp this morning, because he would have had to cover miles, which he could never have done with all the deep snow."

"And, Phil, it must be that he's a Baylay; but we'll find all that out when he comes to himself again in the camp. I'm rested now, so give me a chance to spell you."

Both of them were more pleased than they would have liked to say when they discovered the little shack they had built close to the shore of the lake; with X-Ray just starting out ax in hand to cut some wood.

Ethan gave a whoop, and Lub came running out of the shelter, all excitement.

"Bringing home the bacon, are you, fellows?" he called; "well, you do seem to be staggering under a bully old load, Ethan. Have you bothered getting the moose's head, horns and all to camp? Might have left that hanging up till — well, what's this I see? Great Jehosophat! this isn't a moose's head; it's a child!"

X-Ray was equally astounded. They crowded around, and stared, and seemed ready to fairly burst with curiosity.

"Wait till we get him between blankets, boys, and then you'll have the whole story," said Phil.

Lub rushed in ahead of the others, and it was his blanket that he held up in front of the fire to "get it good and warm for the poor little chap," he explained.

There was more color creeping into the face of the unknown child, Phil discovered. He did not believe anything serious could have come upon him, and hoped for the best.

"I really think he's sleeping from exhaustion and fright now," he told the others, after they had bundled their charge up snugly, and were sitting there before the glowing fire, with both Lub and X-Ray impatiently waiting to hear all about the remarkable occurrence; for it is not often that hunters start out after moose and return bearing a child that they have saved from being frozen to death.

By degrees the story was told, first how the two hunters managed to get close up on the cow moose so that Phil could take a couple of snapshots; and then later on when aiming to discover the beaver village how they had run upon the lad in the thicket, where he had gone to try and make a fire.

"Think of the little duffer having matches in his pocket, and believing he knew all about the job of making a fire, too," said Ethan, as though he considered this the most remarkable feature of the whole thing.

The little toy gun had been carefully carried along with their own larger weapons and Phil held it up as he went on to say:

"And he was trying to find his deer just as much as we were, it seems like, from his having this 'repeater' in his possession. That's why I think he must belong to a backwoodsman or a guide, because children in such families take to doing all these things like ducks do to water."

"And," continued Ethan, solemnly, "so far as we know there's only one party up in this neighborhood who has kids of his own, because you remember Mr. McNab told us about him."

"Gee! you mean that terrible Baylay, don't you?" asked Lub, aghast, as he glanced apprehensively toward the place where the child was snuggled in his blanket, and then toward the adjacent woods.

"Yes, Ethan and myself have about come to the conclusion he must be a chip of the old block, a Baylay, afraid of nothing; though he did bite off more than he could chew when he started off on a hunt for big game in winter time, and found himself lost in the forest, with the snow half way up to his neck in places."

They talked it all over, but no one could suggest any particular thing they could do, save to keep the boy in camp, and wait to see what would turn up.

It came time for them to think of getting supper. X-Ray generously offered to "spell" Lub, for he was afraid they were overdoing it in allowing the stout youth to fill the office of cook continually, and that he might suddenly rebel.

"I don't mind having some help, since you are so kind, X-Ray," Lub told him; "and so the first thing you do fetch me some more wood."

X-Ray had perhaps thought to be the "chief-cook-and-bottle-washer" himself for once, as he himself expressed it, for he made a wry face upon being ordered about in such a summary fashion. However, he nodded his head toward the autocrat of the culinary department, and went off to get his arms full of fuel, saying as he did so:

"Anything to keep peace in the family; and besides I'll have some say about the bill of fare we put up at our hotel this night."

While supper was cooking Ethan caught hold of Phil's sleeve and pointed over to where the little chap had been placed, rolled up in Lub's blanket. He was now sitting bolt upright, and rubbing his eyes with his knuckles as though he did not know what to make of it all.

Phil immediately hurried over, and threw himself down beside the little fellow.

"It's all right, bub, we're your friends, and mean to keep you here with us until your daddy comes along for you. Went out hunting, eh, and got lost? Well, never mind, plenty of bigger men than you have done the same thing. You tried the best you knew how to light a fire, too; and I believe you'd have done it if the ground had been clear of snow, so you could find plenty of small wood. But supper will be ready soon, and we're expecting you to be pretty hungry."

Somehow there was that about Phil Bradley to invite the confidence of any one, especially when he smiled as Phil was doing now, and spoke so soothingly, and directly from the heart.

It was not long before he had the little chap smiling; and when Lub came over into the shelter with a cup of warm soup for the boy, he drank it ravenously. This told Phil that it must have been many hours since the child had tasted any food.

"I wouldn't be surprised if he left his home, wherever that can be, early this morning, and had been pushing his way through the snow ever since. No wonder he was all tired out, and couldn't say a word, but keep on moaning. But he's all right now."

"If they start out and follow his trail," ventured X-Ray, with one of those bright inspirations that had given him his nick-name, "they'll show up here in our camp some time or other, I should say. Whee! I hope now, that terror of the pines will be reasonable, and believe what we tell him; that is, I don't want him to suspect we tried to kidnap Johnny here."

"By the way, I wonder what his name really is?" said Lub.

"Ask him, Phil; he seems to think a heap of you already," suggested X-Ray.

Accordingly Phil bent over the boy, while the others crowded around.

"We want to know whose boy you are, and what your name is, my little man. Do they call you Johnny at home?" he asked, and as clearly as possible.

The small urchin shook his curly head vigorously; he even in a measure returned Phil's smile; and then started to make a series of unintelligible noises that sent a thrill through Phil's heart.

The latter turned with piteous look toward his chums, whose faces reflected his expression of commiseration, almost horror.

"No wonder he didn't say anything, boys!" exclaimed Phil; "for don't you see the poor little chap is tongue-tied?"

CHAPTER X — A RUDE AWAKENING

"The poor little kid!" gasped warm-hearted Lub, as he impulsively threw an arm around the boy they were entertaining as their guest in camp.

Both X-Ray Tyson and Ethan also betrayed their intense interest by sympathetic looks that spoke volumes.

"I don't know that I ever ran across a case just like this," X-Ray remarked, as he turned on Phil.

"You mean that while you've met people who were deaf and dumb you never saw one who was what they call tongue-tied; is that it, X-Ray?" the latter asked.

"Yes, you've got it straight, Phil; but tell me, is this sort of thing incurable?"

"It all depends on the conditions," was the reply. "Some are afflicted worse than others; and then again I believe that if it's taken in hand at an early stage there's much more chance of the operation being successful than if it becomes an old affliction."

"But my stars, why haven't the parents of this fine little chap looked after it before now?" demanded Ethan.

"Well, when you're saying that, just stop and think what you're up against," Phil told him. "We're not down in New York City, where paid doctors visit the poorer sections, and there are wards in all hospitals where such operations can be undertaken free of expense. This is away up in the wilds of Canada."

"Like as not," interrupted Lub, "his folks never dreamed that any remedy could be found to help him get his speech. I reckon now his mammy has grieved her heart sore many a time wondering what would become of a boy growing up to manhood who'd never be able to say a single intelligible word."

"Yes," added Ethan, bent on entering another wedge to the debate, "and money has a heap to do with these things, even if they did know. It costs considerable to send a boy all the way down to Montreal, and keep him there, not to speak of the doctor's big fee."

Phil looked grave, and then a smile began to slowly creep athwart his face. This was discovered by the sharp-eyed X-Ray, for he quickly demanded an explanation.

"You've thought of something, Phil; that look gives you away. Now speak up and confide in your chums. We're all just as much interested in this queer business as you can be, I want you to remember. What's caught you?"

Phil smiled in even a broader sense.

"Why, to be sure you have a right to know, fellows," he told them, frankly. "I'm not intending to keep it a secret. I was just wondering why I shouldn't try and take this little chap down with me when we leave here, and see that he has one good chance to have this impediment to his speech removed. We can go to Montreal without a great deal of trouble; and in fact we had decided that we'd visit there, as we saw Old Quebec on the way up to the Saguenay region. What d'ye think of it?"

"I object!" burst out Lub, to the surprise of his mates.

"Why, what's got you, Lub?" demanded X-Ray, indignantly; "I always thought you'd be the last one to kick up a row, when a thing like this was being talked over."

"I object on the grounds that it isn't fair for Phil to take the burden all on himself," continued the stout chum, resolutely, with his affectionate arm still hovering about the small boy, who had cuddled closer to him, as though recognizing a warm friend in Lub.

"Oh! I haven't said I meant to do that, Lub!" exclaimed Phil.

"Well, we know you too well to believe it wasn't in your mind to stand for every cent of the expense such an operation would cost," continued the fat boy. "Course you wouldn't feel it any more'n a flea-bite; but then that isn't the question. You've got to think of us. We cut some punkins in this arrangement, and we insist on standing our share of any expense. How's that, X-Ray, Ethan?"

"Bully for you, Lub!" ejaculated the former, enthusiastically, slapping the fat chum on the shoulder with almost crushing force that made Lub wince, though he immediately forced a broad smile to dominate his rosy face.

"Share and share alike, that's the ticket!" declared Ethan, though doubtless the poor fellow was at the same time making a rapid mental calculation as to the state of his finances, for he had no private fortune, or rich parents, or doting aunt to help him tide over. "I've got another bundle of ginseng roots ready to ship down to my dealer, and if they fetch anything like the splendid price the last lot did I can spare enough to square my share of the bill. And I'll do it willingly too, if it's the means of giving this little fellow the gift of speech."

There never were four boys quite as generous as Phil Bradley and his chums. Fond of manly sport they were, and full of a love for frolic, and such good times as came their way; but never failing to respond to a call for help, no matter what the source from which the appeal came.

Phil threw up both hands as if in surrender.

"You never will let me do anything like this by myself, fellows," he told them; "even when I've got money to burn. But I want to say right here that I think ten times as much of you, Lub, X-Ray and Ethan, as if you did. It means something to all of you to make this sacrifice, while to me it isn't a bit of difference. So I say and I repeat it, that you deserve a whole lot more credit than I ever can. And what's more, I'm as proud as anything to shake hands with such chums."

He gravely went around pumping a hand of each fellow, and there was a deal of sincerity in the act, even though they all laughed—perhaps to hide the fact that there might be a suspicious moisture in their rapidly winking eyes.

"Isn't it queer how we seem to rub up against something of this kind everywhere we go on our trips?" remarked X-Ray.

"Why, so it is," Ethan added; "in the first place, when we were in the Adirondacks there was that old hermit and his little girl, Mazie; we had a hand in bringing them a measure of joy, and reuniting Meredith with his estranged wife. They've been writing ever since how grateful they were on account of the little we managed to do for them."

"Yes," Lub hurriedly continued, "and even around our home town of Brewster, when we were gathering nuts for the children in the orphan asylum remember how we had a chance to help that country boy, Casper Bunce, who had run away from the farmer he had been bound to. The courts fixed all that, and he's got a happy home now on the farm of Miss Bowers."

"Even down on the Shore, when we were duck shooting on Currituck Sound," X-Ray went on to say, not wishing to be left out entirely, "we managed to bridge over the troubles between the young bayman Malachi Jordon, his little wife, and her savage old dad who was separating the couple. When we left they were all bunched and waving us good-by."

"It does seem to be the bounden duty of the Mountain Boys to carry some sunshine along with them wherever they go," laughed Phil; "and to tell you the truth I'm not so very much surprised."

"You mean it's getting to be a regular thing with us; is that it, Phil?" questioned Lub.

"That's what you might call it, when you keep on repeating a certain thing," Phil declared. "There's an old chestnut of a story you may remember that illustrates the point I'm making. It seems that a lawyer was trying to get a witness to admit a certain point that would favor his side of the case, and the old fellow kept on doggedly avoiding committing himself. So the lawyer asked him what he would call it if he leaned from the window and fell out. 'I'd call that an accident,' replied the witness.

'Then suppose you deliberately walked up-stairs and repeated the identical performance, what would you call that?' demanded the lawyer. 'Oh! I should say that was a coincidence,' the witness told him. 'Well, now what if you even went up again, and for the third time looked out of that same window, only to fall again; what would you call it?' And the witness without the least hesitation bawled out: 'Why, sir, I'd say it was a habit!' And that's what it's getting to be with us Mountain Boys."

Of course they all laughed at Phil's description of the condition into which it seemed they were drifting.

"It's a habit that gives us a heap of lively satisfaction let me tell you," said Lub, earnestly. "For one I like to look back and think of a lot of things we've had a hand in carrying through."

"Yes," said Phil, "we've enjoyed them to the limit, and the best part of it all is that they leave no regrets behind. I hope it will always be that way with the Mountain Boys."

A little later on Phil took his turn at cuddling the small boy up close to him. He was talking to him in a low tone, and the others, knowing what he had in mind, did not bother him, but conversed among themselves of other things.

Presently Phil called softly to Ethan.

"Come and take him off my arm; he's sound asleep, and my arm is too, so I can't move it. Easy now, and lay him down where he'll be the warmest."

"That's where my blanket happens to be," spoke up Lub; "I've figured on having him with me to-night, Phil; so please don't interfere."

"I guess he'll be snug enough alongside such a hot-box as you are, Lub," interrupted X-Ray; and consequently Ethan gently laid the small chap so that Lub's generous blanket could be tucked in around him.

"Did you manage to find out anything worth while, Phil?" asked X-Ray.

"Well, he's some shy yet; and I'm a poor hand at trying to hold a talk-fest with a child that can't say a single word," admitted Phil; "but I'm sure now he does belong to the people we spoke about."

"Meaning that terror of a poacher, Baylay?" said Ethan.

"Yes," Phil continued, "but until we rub up against the man ourselves, and can testify to some of his awful ways, perhaps we'd better go slow about calling him all those names, boys. He may be a rough man, but what more could you expect up here in this wilderness? All loggers are of that stripe. For one I'm going to form my opinion of this Baylay more from how he treats his family, than from his relations to game laws he considers unjust, or other rough men who meet him on the level of give and take."

"I wouldn't be surprised if there was a whole lot of good sense in that policy, Phil," assented Lub, for it agreed with his ideas exactly.

"But he does seem to have gotten a terrible bad reputation around these districts you'll admit?" ventured Ethan.

"There may be two sides to every story," Phil told him; "and so far we've heard only one. I'd like to know just what that kid over yonder thinks of Baylay; then I'd have a better pointer to the true character of the man than I could get from outside talk. He's a fighter, as nearly all these loggers are. He has licked lots of other scrappers in his time, and you couldn't expect them to say nice things about Baylay. So let's hold off a bit, and not condemn him unheard."

Even Ethan admitted that such a course was nothing more than fair.

"We'll wait then," continued Phil, "till the time comes when we can see into his home, and find out if he's a big brute there or not. Yes, that's the way to learn the truth; surface indications don't amount to much. You've got to scratch a man on the back and find out what he does when he's alone, or with his own family, to learn his real nature."

Though the boys may not have known it there was a deal of sound philosophy in what Phil was advancing; and if more people would carry it out there might be less misunderstandings and suffering in this world.

Some time later on they began to feel sleepy themselves, and Lub was the first one to crawl under his covers. Ethan helped him get settled, for the fat chum had to be unusually careful, so as not to awaken his little blanket-mate, who was apparently sleeping soundly.

The night wore on.

Though the wind outside might be cold and bleak the campers had managed to fix things so well that little of it could find entrance to their shack. The fire was to be allowed to take care of itself, unless one of the boys chanced to wake up in the night, and chose to crawl out in order to throw more fuel on the embers.

It is not the most pleasant task in the world to do a thing like this on a bitter cold night, when all seems so comfortable under the covers. Even Phil might conclude to let it pass, since a fire was so easy to start in the morning, and he could have a merry blaze going long before any of the rest thought of sticking their noses out.

No doubt Lub, and perhaps the others also, dreamed of home as they lay there so many hundreds of miles away from those they loved. It would have been only natural, because their thoughts often dwelt with the distant scenes, even though they might be enjoying every hour of their vacation in Canadian wilds.

If any of them awoke they had no means of telling how the night was passing unless they cared to peep out and note the position of the planets, those telltale clocks of the skies. All of the boys had paid more or less attention to such things, knowing how useful the knowledge can be when there is no watch in the party; and many times they had vied with one another in seeing who could display the better judgment in explaining where certain bright stars would be at a designated hour.

Lub was lying squarely on his back, and breathing so hard that some of his comrades would have reproached him for "snoring" had they heard him. But Lub seemed to be far away in his dreams, and not concerning himself in the slightest degree as to whether he emitted little snorts or not.

From this happy condition, so free from care, the fat boy was suddenly and rudely aroused by a terrifying sound. It was a shout, and undoubtedly came from the throat of X-Ray, who could elevate his voice in a shrill manner that few of his friends could ever hope of emulating. He was the cheer captain of their school football squad in Brewster, just on that account.

And what he now shouted was not calculated to cheer the hearts of his comrades but to send a pang of fear through every fiber of their being:

"Hello! hello! rouse up everybody! Our shack's on fire!"

CHAPTER XI—ON GUARD

Everybody was awake in an instant. Even though the cry had thrilled Lub through and through somehow he did not seem to forget about the little fellow who was under the covers with him; for his very first act was to lift him up, blanket and all, and struggle to get out of the shack.

They had all seen a light, though it had remained for the keen eyes of X-Ray to discover what caused it. But as soon as they emerged from the shelter, Phil, Ethan and Lub found no difficulty in seeing that the alarm had not been a false one; for one side of the shack was all afire.

"Go for it, everybody!" cried Phil, as he started to throw all the snow he was able to snatch up on the fiercely burning mass.

"Fire-fighters get busy!" echoed X-Ray, copying the other's example; nor was Lub long in finding a place where he could deposit his burden and join in the attack.

Thus beset on all sides the fire quickly died down as the snow melted and drowned the ardor of the flames. Before many minutes had passed away they had it under control.

"We want to save a part of it for our regular fire, because we'll need it to get warm by!" observed long-headed Ethan.

"Warm!" gasped Lub. "Why, I'm fairly roasting right now."

"Well, you won't be in a jiffy, when that cold wind strikes down your back," the other warned him; "how about the fire business, Phil?"

"It's a good idea," he was told; "but don't bother carrying any of what is left of this stuff over; we have plenty of good wood handy, you remember. And I want to look a little closer into this brush-heap, you see."

"Ginger popguns; that's so," cried X-Ray; "however did that stuff get there, I'd like to know? We didn't bank it up that I remember."

"Never mind about that yet," Phil told him; "get the fire going, and then we can talk it over. There's something about this affair that looks pretty suspicious to me, I want you to know."

All of them were thinking the same thing as they hurried to get their own fire going in front of the shack.

When this had been accomplished they found time to look around. The boy was sitting up, and Lub had seen to it that he had the warm folds of the blanket about him, so he was in no danger of taking cold. He looked both puzzled and full of wonder, but Phil noticed that he did not appear to be afraid.

"He's made of good stuff, most likely," he told himself; "and is a chip off the old block all right, if he's Baylay's boy; because they admit the poacher is a man without fear."

"Now," remarked Ethan, after they were all seated near the fire, "let's try and get a little light on this mystery. How did that fire come to be started; and who put all that brush up against the back of our shack, I want to know?"

"That's so, who did?" echoed Lub, wagging his head with the words, and looking unusually solemn.

"Notice in the first place," Phil continued, "that it was piled up on the windward side; that was done so it would take hold in a hurry, once the match was struck. I even got a whiff of kerosene when I was working at putting out the blaze; and it strikes me some of it was used over the brush to make it burn more furiously."

"Whee!" gasped Lub; "then you mean to say, Phil—"

"I mean that this thing didn't come about by accident," the other interrupted Lub to say positively; "none of us put that stuff there, and we have no kerosene to waste throwing it around. Besides, every one was sound asleep inside the shack when it happened."

"Somebody meant to burn us out, that's it, Phil!" declared X-Ray.

"Baylay?" cried Ethan, on a hazard.

"Not on your life," X-Ray told him; "Baylay doesn't know there are any such fellows as the Mountain Boys on earth. But there is one man who does, because he ran up against a couple of the same latterly, and had to duck. I'm referring to the eminent capitalist and financier millionaire, Mr. James Bodman."

"Whee!" breathed Lub again, as his emotions almost overpowered him; he did not venture to interrupt, but just sat there and listened with all his might to the exciting talk that was going on among his chums.

"Well," said Ethan, slowly, "from the description of that sportsman, and the way he acted when he found he couldn't bulldoze the pair of you, I wouldn't put a thing like this past him; but how would he know where we were camped?"

"Oh! that is easy to answer," Phil told him; "don't you remember how we learned where they were settled by seeing smoke rising in the cold air, straight as a church pillar?"

"I reckon they could see the same if they happened to look this way," admitted Ethan, "because Lub uses all kinds of wood, and some of it makes a black smudge. Well, I'll admit for the sake of argument that they could easy enough learn where our camp lay; but do you believe that stout sportsman would go to the trouble to sneak all the way over here, several miles it must be, just to try and make us some nasty mean trouble?"

"No, I don't," replied Phil, instantly.

"Then what follows?" demanded the other, desperately.

"He knows the power of money, because he uses it right along to further some of his big schemes," Phil exclaimed.

"You mean he could bribe a couple of his guides to come over here and do the burning racket; is that what you have in mind, Phil?" asked Ethan.

"Yes, there's no doubt of it in my mind," he was told.

"But we'd always have to just guess at it, because we could never know for sure," X-Ray went on to say, in a dubious tone that told of disappointment.

"Perhaps not," Phil remarked; "come over with me, and let's take a look; for I've got a notion we can settle that thing in our minds, even if nothing might ever be done to punish the sneaks who did the job."

He picked up a burning brand from the fire that promised to serve fairly well as a torch; and with this swinging from his hand led the others to the back of the scorched shack.

"Close by we've all trodden things into a mass," he explained; "but let's look further away. Here's a place where it happens we find only a couple of inches of snow, and you can see footprints plainly marked. Look again, and tell me if any of us made those tracks coming and going?"

"They carried the brush along here, too, Phil, because you can see little twigs lying on the surface of the snow!" announced Ethan.

"But examine the footprints, because they will tell the story," said Phil.

"Why, they are not like our tracks at all," said X-Ray, immediately.

"None of them show any sign of heels, Phil!" exclaimed Ethan; "does that mean they can be moccasins made of tough hide, and not hunting-boots like ours?"

"Now you're getting close to the heart of it," the leader assured him; "for most of the guides up here in this region wear such foot coverings, as the Indians did before them. I believe there were two men concerned in this outrage, and that they were paid by Mr. James Bodman to come over here and burn us out."

"The coward!" muttered Lub, indignantly, as his pent-up feelings broke bounds; "why, they might have smothered us while we slept."

"Oh! I don't suppose the millionaire believed it would be as bad as that, for I hardly think he's got to the point where he'd commit murder outright;

but he meant to give us all the bother he could. That was his way of trying to get even because we refused to knuckle down to him, and let him claim our caribou."

"Huh! guess then he's been crazy to shoot game like that for a long time; and was a whole heap disappointed when he found it was our shots that had downed the young buck," and X-Ray chuckled as though he felt that after all the score was still decidedly in their favor.

"What surprises me, and makes me feel small," continued Phil, "is how I could sleep through it all and never know that they were creeping up, fetching that brush along with them, and piling it against the back of the shack."

"Oh! we're all in the same boat," said Ethan, "because I was hundreds of miles away from here, and going to singing school with Sally Andrews when X-Ray let out that yawp!"

"And I own up that it was just by a lucky chance I happened to wake up," X-Ray Tyson admitted; "you know smoke always makes me choke, and that's why I try to sit on the windward side of fires. It must have got in my throat as I slept, because I suddenly sat upright to get my breath. Course I knew right away something was on the boards that ought to be attended to, and so I woke the rest up gently."

"Gently!" echoed Lub; "say, it seemed to me as if an electric current heavy enough to execute a criminal had been shot through my system. I bet you I've lost as much as five pounds in weight just through the nervous excitement."

"Poor chap!" said X-Ray; "it's a pity then it doesn't happen oftener. I think I'll take to giving you a regular shock like that every few nights. You could drop forty pounds and be all the better for it."

"Who's running my heft, me or you, I want to know?" demanded Lub; "it suits me just as it is. When I get a notion that I want to start to join your

Living Skeleton class I'll give you due notice. And until that time comes please let me sleep in peace."

"Well, what can we do about this outrage?" asked Ethan.

"Nothing much," admitted Phil.

"It would be silly to think of going over and entering a complaint to that red-faced grunter," declared X-Ray; "because we'd only be insulted to our faces. Why I wouldn't put it past him to threaten to have us kicked out of his camp, though of course James would have too much sense to try the job himself."

"We'll have to pocket the insult, and try to guard against having it happen again, that's all," was Phil's conclusion. "And let me tell you we have to be thankful it turned out no worse than it did. The damage isn't worth mentioning, and it's opened our eyes to the fact that we have dangerous neighbors who will bear watching from this time out."

"But, Phil, we don't mean to let them chase us away from here, do we?" interposed Lub, who came of good Revolutionary stock, and was a sticker.

"Well, I guess not, if we have to keep on the watch every single night," retorted X-Ray, belligerently.

"Are we going to sit here till it's time to get breakfast?" asked Lub, casting a solicitous glance over toward the spot where the boy was wrapped in his blanket—it would be hard to say whether Lub were concerned about the welfare of the little fellow, or coveted the warmth of the said blanket; perhaps he might have been influenced by both motives, for his heart was warm, even when he shivered with the cold breeze on his back.

"No use of that, when it's hardly an hour after midnight right now!" declared Phil, with a look aloft to where the star-studded sky gave him the information. "The rest of you toddle back to the shack and let me sit here a while," Ethan told them, as he gathered his blanket closer about him, after picking up his gun, as Phil noticed.

"I was just going to say the same thing myself, Ethan," remarked the leader.

"But first come, first served, that's the rule we go by, remember, Phil."

"I'll agree, on one condition," he was told.

"Name it then, Phil."

"There's Jupiter away up yonder; in just about two hours he'll be setting below the horizon. Promise to call me before he disappears from sight, will you, Ethan."

"Agreed, though I wouldn't mind sticking out the watch till daylight," said the other, and his manner told that he certainly meant every word of it.

"But how about me?" complained X-Ray; "there's another star up yonder that will set by five o'clock; you've got to promise to let me stand guard from then on to daylight. I refuse to be left out in the cold in any deal."

"And don't I have any show at all?" whined Lub, though rather faintly, as though he knew very well they would not consent; for he had a failing with respect to going to sleep on his post, having been tested on numerous occasions and found wanting.

It was presently arranged then that Phil would arouse X-Ray when the second star was about to disappear. He smiled faintly when making this concession, but X-Ray did not appear to notice it. The fact of the matter was Phil knew very well that there had been a serious miscalculation on the part of the ambitious sentinel, because that second star would still be half an hour from the horizon when the sun was due to send his flaming banners athwart the eastern sky to herald his approach.

The fire had scorched the back of their shelter but no serious damage had been accomplished. That was owing to the fact of smoke affecting the sensitive throat of X-Ray Tyson; a thing that may have caused him more or less discomfort in times past, but which certainly stood them all in good stead on this particular night.

On this account they could sleep just as well as before, granting of course that their nerves had not been too much disturbed by the sudden peril, and the fight they had had to put up in order to save their possessions.

The fire was now to be kept up without intermission, day and night. Should any of those unprincipled men come over again from the other camp, bent on doing them an injury, they might well pause and abandon the attempt when they discovered how the boys maintained a constant watch, with arms in their hands, and sufficient light to discover a creeping figure, which they would be justified in firing at.

True to his promise Ethan aroused Phil when Jupiter was about to dip behind the horizon.

"All well, and getting colder right along, so that the fire feels bully!" was all the report the late sentry thought fit to make, after he had seen Phil take his place on the log, gun in hand, and blanket about his shoulders.

"Then crawl in, and go to sleep," advised the new guard, as he watched Ethan trying to smother a huge yawn.

"Guess I will, because it's quite some time to daylight, and there's little use for a pair of us to stand sentry duty."

So Ethan vanished inside the shack, and Phil was left to insure their safety, as the brilliant heavenly bodies kept up their steady western march, and the night breeze sang mysterious chants through the snow-covered branches of the firs.

CHAPTER XII – LAYING PLANS

"Is that the way you keep a promise, Phil?" asked X-Ray, reproachfully, as he came crawling out of the shack, to find it beginning to get daylight, and with the sentry busying himself before a cheery fire, where he meant evidently to forestall Lub in starting breakfast.

"Oh! the joke is on you, that's all," laughed Phil.

"I don't see how," complained X-Ray, who really felt hurt in that he had not been allowed to stand his share of the night watch after being told he might.

"You'll have to learn to figure better, that's all, my boy," the other told him.

"Figure; how's that, Phil?"

"Well, learn to judge distances that are millions of miles away, to be more definite. Look over there to the west; see that star just going down? Well, that's the one you told me would set in two hours after Jupiter disappeared. I've been watching it right along, and somehow it just refused to vanish. There, I believe it's just dropped out of sight. If you were asleep, X-Ray, I'd think it my duty to go and get you on deck, because I promised I would."

X-Ray looked a bit foolish, and then laughed.

"Another time I'll see to it that I'm Johnny on the spot!" he declared. "Chances are you knew I'd figured wrong at the time, Phil?"

"What if I did, it wasn't in the bond that I should take you to task for that blunder. A little thing of this kind is going to impress it on your mind better than any words of mine could ever do. You'll never forget again to prove your sums so as to make doubly sure."

And Phil was right. X-Ray would never look up at the stars and try to figure on how long it would be before a certain one would set, without remembering his error of judgment, and taking especial pains that it was not repeated.

The others soon made their appearances, hearing this talking outside.

"Whew! but it's sharp this morning!" exclaimed Ethan as he joined them. "That blanket of mine isn't as warm as it might be, and I don't believe it's all wool and two yards wide. Where's the ax?"

"Going to cut some wood so as to get warm?" asked X-Ray Tyson.

"What, me?" cried Ethan, pretending to scoff at the idea; "why, fact is I want to chop a hole in the lake ice, and take a bath just to get my blood in circulation. They say there's nothing like it, you know."

All the same, after he had picked up one of the axes he was found to be cutting wood, which proved his daring assertion that had made Lub gasp to be pretty much in the nature of a great "bluff."

The boy was sitting by the fire where Lub had found him a place. Lub had insisted on Phil giving over the completion of breakfast into his charge.

"I've been elected chief cook by unanimous vote," he said, as he waved a big spoon about his head to emphasize his assertion; "and I expect you all to do what I tell you."

So he set them each one a task, Phil "spelling" Ethan at the woodpile, X-Ray to fetch plenty of fuel up, and Ethan something else when he had recovered his wind after his recent violent exertions.

As he cooked the breakfast Lub talked confidentially to the boy, who was looking quite contented and happy, as indeed who would not when finding such good friends, and being treated to such bountiful spreads?

"Are we going to try and take him back to his mammy to-day, Phil?" asked Ethan, later on, as they sat on the log, and discussed the eggs and bacon and coffee and flapjacks which had been produced so bountifully under the deft manipulation of the obliging Lub.

"Oh! what's the hurry?" the cook hastened to say; "it's threatening again, you can notice if you look at that bank of storm clouds coming up yonder.

Better put it off a while. We've got oceans of grub, you know; and I like to feel him wrapped up in a blanket with me first-rate."

All of them looked to Phil to give the deciding word, though as a rule he always consulted his chums before saying anything, and tried to have it so that majority ruled the camp.

"I quite agree with Lub," he went on to say, quietly, as he gave that individual a smile, and then nodded his head toward the little chap.

"Good for you, Phil!" burst out Lub, clapping his hands together in delight.

"I don't altogether like the looks of things over there where those clouds are coming up," continued Phil. "It wouldn't be the nicest thing in the world to try to take this boy miles away, and then get caught in a howling blizzard. We'd do better to hold our horses and see what turns up."

"Oh! then you expect that some one may come along looking for him, do you?" asked X-Ray, jumping to conclusions.

"It's possible," he was told. "If they care at all for the child, when he's missed it seems to me there would be some stir; and one of the first things that ought to occur to his father would be to notify any campers around here, so they could be on the lookout for the kid as they trailed through the bush."

"Phil is right," asserted Ethan Allen, hastily. "It's sure up to Baylay to get a move on him and do something, if he's lost his boy. He couldn't expect to stay at home and wait for others to find the lost child."

"We don't know," said Phil, "but the chances are the mother and father have been pretty near being distracted because by now they must feel there's no chance of the kid being alive, unless he was picked up by a roving hunter or trapper."

The boy listened to all they said, though of course it was not likely that he understood much of it. He could see nothing but friendly smiles on each one of the four faces by the fire; and he knew as well as anything could be known that his lines had fallen in pleasant places.

When this matter had been settled all of them seemed to be relieved of a weight. The fact of the matter was they had already taken a great fancy to the waif, and like Lub none of them wanted to see him depart.

It did begin to blow and snow heavily ere another hour had passed. X-Ray declared that from the signs they were in for a fierce blizzard; and he told some fearful stories he had read concerning these dreadful storms.

Lo! and behold the treacherous weather played him a sly trick, for the sun came out even while he was in the midst of the most doleful yarn, and his chums gave him a merry laugh in consequence.

At the same time there was enough of threat in the clouds to keep them in camp that morning, finding plenty to do to employ their time.

In prowling around Phil had made several little discoveries concerning the abiding places or haunts of certain small fur-bearing animals that frequented the border of the lake. His collection of flashlight pictures was lacking in some particulars, and he believed it would pay him to commence work trying to obtain results while on the spot.

"I wouldn't want to go back home without a few additions to my splendid series of flash exposures," he told the others while getting things ready so that he could place his cunning little trap when the shadows of evening began to gather; "and I want to see if the animals up here in this half Arctic region are as obliging as they are down in our section of the country, so as to take their own pictures for a poor hard worked photographer who needs sleep, and can't afford to sit up all night just to press a button and fire the cartridge."

"You always make it a paying business for the victim, Phil," declared Lub; "for you give him a jolly lunch to settle for his trouble. Huh! seems to me I'd like to just pull a string and get a flash if only it meant grub every time, and no harm done. They're a lucky lot, I'll be bound."

Lub had taken a turn during the morning in trying to talk with the tongue-tied boy. Of course it could only be done through the use of many signs, although there was always a chance that the little chap might know a name if he heard it.

"When I kept repeating the word Baylay I could see that he seemed interested," Lub told the others. "It's too bad we didn't ask Mr. McNab what the names of the Baylay kids were. I've tried every one I could think of and none seemed to fit. He shook his curly head every time as if he wanted me to know he owned to no such name. I reckon now they must be out of the ordinary."

And it afterwards turned out that Lub was quite right when he chanced to make this assertion, for the boy's name was indeed out of the ordinary; so it was no wonder Lub failed to strike it in his vocabulary.

Noon came and found things just about as before.

Some of them had been half expecting to see a bulky figure pushing toward the camp; but the hours had crept on without such a thing coming to pass.

"It's too late now to think of starting out to try and find the place where the Baylay cabin is located," asserted Ethan, when the afternoon was fairly well advanced, and the clouds seemed to have given up the battle for supremacy, for they were retreating all along the line, leaving a cold blue sky in evidence instead.

"Of course it is," Lub hastened to add, a wrinkle making its appearance across his forehead, a "pucker" Ethan always called it, and which was apt to show whenever the fat chum became worried over something or other.

The quick look he took in the direction of his charge explained the cause on this particular occasion. Lub always was fond of kids, and they loved him too. In this case the fact of their visitor being a waif of the snow forest had more or less to do with his feelings; and then, besides, the poor little chap being unable to do more than make those distressing sounds when he did want to express his feelings the worst kind brought a pang to Lub's tender heart.

"Yes," Phil decided, "it would be foolish to attempt anything of the kind now. It can wait until morning. They've given up all hope by now, I'm afraid, so they'll not be apt to suffer much worse for a little more delay. And getting the boy back safe and sound will make them all the happier."

"That's the way it treats me always," affirmed Lub, looking inexpressibly relieved at hearing the dictum pronounced that meant another night with his little blanket-mate; "I never wanted a thing real bad, and kept being put off and put off but that it got to be what my mother would call an absorbing passion with me."

"Yes, just like the baby in the bath leaning over and trying to reach a cake of well known soap, you'd 'never be happy till you got it,' eh, Lub?" jeered X-Ray.

"It's contradiction that makes men great," said Lub, ponderously. "Difficulties bring out all there is in a fellow, and Phil will tell you so too. The life that flows on calmly never amounts to much. That's what makes these mountaineers such a hardy lot; they have to fight for everything they get, while the people on the fertile plains make an easy living."

"Gee! listen to the philosopher talk, will you?" said Ethan, pretending to be much surprised, when in truth he knew very well that once in so often Lub was apt to drop into this moralizing mood, and air some pretty bright views, for the benefit of his comrades in arms.

"No trouble now telling where that other camp is," X-Ray informed them. "All you have to do is to take a glance over that way, and you'll see a thick black smoke rising up."

"If we'd had any idea there'd be trouble lying in wait for us around here," ventured Ethan, "we might have kept them guessing where we had our camp. It would be easy to pick out good dry wood, of which there is plenty lying around, and using only that kind. It gives out so little smoke they never would have noticed; whereas the half-green stuff tells anybody with half an eye where the fire is."

"What you say about the wood and the smoke is all very true, Ethan," remarked Phil; "but all the same I doubt whether it would have prevented their finding our location, once Mr. James Bodman started to make things interesting by offering a bonus to his guides to smell us out. They'd have heard us chopping, it might be, for in these still woods sounds carry a long ways when the air is just right."

"Yes, I guess that's so," X-Ray admitted, "because several times I've been positive I heard the sound of a faraway ax at work; and I noticed that the wind was coming from that quarter too."

"To-night we keep watch as we planned, eh, Phil?" Ethan asked.

"We'd be wise to do it just as long as we expect to hang out around this section, and that crowd is over there," he was informed.

"Yes, and I ought to be given the first watch, because I managed to get off so slick last night," asserted X-Ray; "promise me that, won't you?"

"If it's going to worry you the sooner we say yes the better," laughed Phil; "so we'll consider that the night is to be cut up into thirds, and I choose the second watch for my turn; Ethan, you have to tag on at the end."

"So long as I get my full share of the work it doesn't matter a bit to me where I come in; but let there be no tricks on travelers played to-night. What's fair for one is fair to all."

"I suppose you mean to count me out, as usual?" complained Lub, feebly protesting.

"You have all you can do attending to the grub question," said X-Ray, sternly. "If you do happen to wake up in the night, and can't get to sleep again, why you might employ yourself fixing up in your mind some new dish you want to spring on us as a surprise. But as a sentry, wide awake and vigilant, you know you're a rank fizzle, Lub. Now please don't fire up, and want particulars, because I'd hate to rake up bygone happenings."

"Oh! well, if you're three to one against me there's no use in my kicking," admitted Lub, trying to look only resigned, whereas in spite of him a grin would persist in spreading across one side of his rosy features.

He had done his duty in showing a willingness to take part in the protection of the camp; if his chums were a unit in deciding against him having a share in the sitting-up business he could not say anything more.

"Your part to-night will be to see that our little friend here is kept cozy and warm," Phil told him, as he patted the boy on his curly head, and was surprised when the little fellow in the gratitude of his heart suddenly seized hold of his hand and actually pressed it to his childish lips.

Never would Phil Bradley forget the sensation he experienced upon receiving mute evidence of affection; it drew him more than ever to the hapless one whom affliction had marked for its own in refusing him the great gift of speech.

"Hello! listen to all that row going over there, will you?" cried X-Ray Tyson.

As they started up with strained ears there came floating on the wind faint but unmistakable sounds that somehow thrilled the listeners through and through.

CHAPTER XIII — THE MYSTERY OF THE PINE WOODS

"What in the dickens can it all mean?" exclaimed Ethan Allen.

"I'm all up in the air about it," admitted Lub, helplessly.

"I heard several shots from guns!" declared X-Ray Tyson, positively enough.

"Yes, we all did," affirmed Phil; "and there was a howl in the bargain that sounded to me like that of a dog."

"Whew! I bet you one of their animals has gone mad, and had to be shot!" burst out Lub, in still further excitement.

"What, at this season of the year?" cried X-Ray; "I thought curs only went mad in the heat of summer, and that was why they called a part of August the dog days."

"That isn't a fact, is it, Phil?" appealed Lub.

"They used to think so," came the reply, "but of late it's been learned that the heat has little if anything to do with a dog going mad. Because they always run with their tongues hanging out people had an idea the heat affected them. On the contrary the very sight of water causes a mad dog to go into spasms. It's just a terrible disease, and in cities is said to be more frequent in winter than in summer."

"The racket has died out now," remarked X-Ray, partly to change the subject, and hide the little confusion he felt at displaying his ignorance in his little dispute with Lub.

"And I guess the dog has been killed," Ethan went on to remark; "but it took a whole lot of gunning to do the job, seemed like. They must have been pretty badly rattled, those New York City sportsmen who are up here to run the country about as they see fit."

"I'd like to have seen the affair," observed X-Ray Tyson, meditatively, as if he might be trying to draw a mental picture of what must have been an exciting episode; for a mad dog in camp is likely to create considerable of a wild stampede.

"Excuse me from that sort of fun," Lub protested; "I'm too fond of dogs to want to watch one running around, frothing at the mouth, and having to be executed."

"Shot down like a dog, you mean," interposed Ethan; "and I wouldn't be much surprised if that old saying originated in a mad dog scare."

All seemed quiet and serene once more over in the direction of the other camp. Whatever the cause of all that shooting and shouting may have been, it had become a thing of the past, apparently.

"Well, it isn't any of our funeral," X-Ray remarked, with a queer shrug of his shoulders; "and so I guess we'd better forget all about it."

Lub noticed that Phil did not seem to agree with the last speaker. He had a serious expression on his face that told of some idea forming in his brain.

"Perhaps it wasn't a mad dog scare after all," Phil suggested.

"But what else could it have been?" asked Ethan.

"Those sort of sportsmen always fetch lots of liquor along with them into the woods," asserted Phil; "and it might be one of them had a fit ofdelirium tremens, so that he even tried to shoot up the camp, and had to be restrained."

"Well, now, there might be something in that," admitted X-Ray, nodding his head reflectively. "And p'raps right now they've got a badly wounded man over there, with no doctor inside of a hundred miles."

"I was thinking of that," ventured Phil; and something in his tone and manner caused Ethan to instantly leap to a conclusion.

"Were you figuring on going over that way, Phil?" he demanded, "and offering to help that tough crowd if they needed any assistance, you knowing so much about looking after gunshot hurts that we often threatened to call you Doctor Bradley?"

"Yes, I was considering doing that," Phil said, smiling, "though there might be no necessity for our entering the camp, if we seemed to find it all serene."

"I take note of the fact," continued Ethan, "that you use the plural pronoun 'we,' Phil, which would indicate that you meant to have one of us go along. I'd like to speak for that privilege, if it's all the same to you."

"Shucks! you beat me out in saying that, hang the luck, Ethan," grumbled X-Ray Tyson, who was not often caught napping, and therefore felt additionally sore in connection with this instance.

"Yes, if we think it a wise thing to do, you might as well help me out, Ethan," Phil told him; at which the Allen boy grinned happily, and could not keep from casting a side look full of triumph toward X-Ray.

"I don't see that it could do any harm," Lub advanced in his ponderous way, "if you scouted in that direction. You wouldn't have to brush in on them unless you saw signs that they were all mixed up, and in need of the right kind of help. And like as not you'd easily enough be able to find out what all the row was about, so as to tell us stay-at-homes."

"Come on, let's go, Phil?"

Somehow the idea seemed to appeal more and more to Ethan as he thought it over. The other camp was only a couple of miles, more or less, away, and on their snow-shoes they could make it in what the boys would call "double-quick" order.

Phil looked up at the sky. It was only a part of his customary caution, and not that he really expected there would be any signs of trouble in that quarter.

"All right, then, Ethan; get your gun and your snow-shoes. We'll take that scout and see if we can find out anything worth while."

"I hope both of you keep your eyes smartly about you while you're passing along through the woods," urged Lub. "A mad dog is a terrible thing to run across; and for all we know the beast might have got away."

"Ten to one, Phil," sang out Ethan, with a carefree laugh, "poor old timid Lub here will spend every minute of the time we're away sitting on a log by the fire with his gun on his lap, and ready to whack away at any suspicious four-legged beast that shows up."

"Well, can you blame me?" demanded the stout boy; "I read about a fellow who was bitten by a mad dog, and it's haunted me ever since. I guess I'd rather be taken prisoner by hostile Indians, and burned at the stake, than bitten by a dog suffering with the rabies."

He stepped over and securing his gun found a comfortable spot on the log near the fire. Here he drew the small waif close to his left side, and looked as though he meant to stay there in that one position as long as two of the guardians of the shack were absent on their risky errand.

Phil only loitered a couple of minutes to snatch up his camera. There could be no telling when he might run across a chance to make use of this. It is like a gun in that respect, for you often see the most marvelous pictures when you have unfortunately left the camera at home.

They started off with the best wishes of those left behind.

"Course you've thought to put your little medicine-case in your pocket, Phil?" sang out Lub; "it came in mighty handy down on the Coast, when we found that young bayman doubled up with pain, after eating some canned stuff that gave him a little touch of ptomaine poisoning; yes I can see it bulging out on the left side of your coat. Well, so-long; and hurry back, because the night isn't so far away, and supper will be cooking, you know."

The two boys made a bee-line for the other camp. Both of them remembered its location, from having taken note of the column of smoke so often. Ethan was doing better work with his snow-shoes right along now, for there is nothing that serves one so well in this respect as practice.

They had covered the first mile with ease.

"Must be all of half way there, Phil?" suggested Ethan.

"Yes."

"And do we keep straight on as we're going now, or make a little detour so as to come on the camp from the other side?" continued Ethan.

Phil smiled.

"I see you're up to all the little dodges of the profession, Ethan," he chuckled, "and are bound to make an A Number One tracker yet. Yes, we might as well begin to circle some from here on, always keeping in mind the point we're aiming to reach."

"No trouble at all about locating the camp, Phil, as long as they continue to burn that half-green wood."

"It does send up a pile of black smoke for a fact," admitted Phil, looking in the direction his chum was pointing; "and we'll keep an eye on it as we go."

Of course as they made progress through the bush the boys did not neglect to observe everything around them. Lub's solemn warning may not have made much of an impression on their minds, but habit proved strong, with Phil at least, and it was his custom to be on the alert.

"We're getting in close now," whispered Ethan; "I thought I heard a cough, then."

"That's right, and I can see the fire beyond that thick bunch of pines," was what the other replied, in the same low tone.

Still advancing cautiously they gradually reached a spot where they were able to look in on the rival camp. The fire was burning, but things seemed to be rather quiet. At least the two scouts failed to discover any furious rushing to and fro that would indicate excitement and alarm.

"Looks peaceful enough, Phil, doesn't it?" whispered Ethan, in rather a disappointed fashion, that would indicate he had felt hopeful the services of his chum might be needed, and that they could thus heap coals of fire on the head of the boastful and vindictive Mr. James Bodman, millionaire sportsman.

"There's one of the guides near the fire," remarked Phil.

"Yes, and he seems to be rather upset over something," pursued Ethan; "notice how he keeps on looking to the right and to the left. See him start to hold up his hands then, will you? What in the wide world can have been going on over here?"

"Seems like a mystery," admitted Phil, still staring at the vicinity of the camp fire where only that one guide was visible.

"Where d'ye suppose the others all are?" ventured Ethan, keeping his voice down to the lowest possible pitch, although there did not seem to be any reason for such caution.

"I suppose in those two shacks we see," came the hesitating answer; and then the other heard Phil give a little gasp.

"You've discovered something; what is it?" Ethan asked, eagerly.

"They did shoot a dog, it seems, Ethan!"

"How do you know?" continued the other, craning his neck to look.

"You can see it lying there over by the woodpile," Phil told him.

"Great Cæsar! so it is, and with his feet up in the air. It's a dead dog, Phil; no fooling about that."

"Yes, and has been shot, but who did it we don't know yet, Ethan."

"Whew! I wonder if he bit that ugly red-faced sportsman you told us about, Phil? I don't wish my worst enemy to meet with such a fate, it would seem as if it might be a judgment on that bully and railroad wrecker if he did get a good scare."

"Queer where the rest of the party are?" continued Phil; "let's creep along this way a bit. We may get to a place where we can glimpse them."

"There may have been another dog that got away, and the rest are hunting for him in the bush right now?" suggested Ethan; but the supposition could not have struck Phil very strongly for he made no comment.

They made their way along as silently as they could. The soughing of the wind through the tops of the pines and the larches and the firs deadened any little scratching sound their snow-shoes may have made as they moved onward.

It was while they were making this change of base that suddenly without the slightest warning Phil laid his hand on the arm of his companion, and at the same time drew him down behind some bushes.

When the startled Ethan turned his eyes upon Phil he saw that the other had a finger pressed upon his lips. This indicated additional caution. It also meant that silence was desirable for some reason or other, which of course Ethan could not immediately fathom.

Then he saw Phil gradually raise his head. He was looking carefully over the tops of the bushes at something. Ethan, quivering with suspense, could hardly restrain his natural impulse to follow suit; and fortunately for his peace of mind Phil just then made a gesture with his hand as though inviting him to join him.

As Ethan did so he saw his chum extend his hand with a pointed finger. Looking on a line with this latter digit he made a discovery.

Something was moving near by. In place of a giant tree that had succumbed to the tempest many years previously, there had grown up a bunch of suckers, and some five of these offshoots had become quite good-sized trunks. They were arranged very much like the fingers and thumb of a partly-closed hand, so that there was a cup which the five protecting trunks surrounded.

It was just a natural hiding place, and apparently some one was even then occupying the cup; for as Ethan looked he saw a head projected, and held there for a dozen seconds, to be withdrawn, and then almost immediately come into view again.

Whoever the party might be he evidently had his whole attention taken up with watching the camp, as though it might hold something that had an important bearing on his condition of happiness and peace of mind.

"He's spying on the camp, Phil!" whispered Ethan, in the other's ear.

"Looks like it," murmured Phil.

"Can it be your fire-eater of a Baylay, then?" was the next thing Ethan suggested.

"Hardly," replied Phil. "This man is afraid; his every action tells that he's been in a big panic lately, and hasn't recovered."

"Go on, Phil?" urged the other, eager to know what next his chum would say.

"I think I know who he must be, Ethan."

"Good. Tell me then, Phil."

"Now watch again when he pokes out and take notice of what sort of a thing he's got on his head."

"There he comes once more, and he certainly does act like a man who's afraid. But what's this I see? Makes me think of the chef in a hotel; for he's wearing a white cap without a peak!"

"Well, that's just what he is, the chef these railroad magnates have fetched up with them to give them the best of meals while in camp," whispered Phil.

"But whatever can he be doing hiding that way, and acting as if he was in mortal fear of his life? If you've got an idea please tell me, Phil."

CHAPTER XIV — MR. JAMES BODMAN GIVES A DANCE

"I'm as much in the dark as you can be, Ethan," Phil told him.

"It's mighty queer, I say; and I'd give something to know what it means," muttered the other scout, who evidently had more than his allotted share of curiosity.

Phil seemed to be debating as to whether it was enough of their business to pay them for taking any more trouble. The only thing that tempted him in that direction was the chance that some one might have been injured during all that shooting, and he would like to be useful in an emergency. All right-minded people who go into the woods feel that way toward others.

"Well, let's creep up and interview the cook!" he suggested.

At that Ethan grinned as though greatly pleased.

"Sure thing, Phil!" he whispered.

They immediately started to carry out this plan. Phil kept his gun in evidence, and Ethan followed suit. This was not to be taken so much in the nature of a threat as an inducement to awaken confidence in the terrified chef. If he saw that they were also hunters he might feel disposed to remain where he was, and satisfy their curiosity, at least to a reasonable extent.

After more or less of shifting of their line of advance to meet the various conditions that arose, they found themselves close in upon the bunch of trees. And apparently the man who was hiding must have caught some little sound just then, for on turning his head he saw them.

Phil guessed he must be a little Frenchman even before he heard him give utterance to a single word, just from his appearance, and the tiny black mustache he sported. He was dressed in white, and they might not have noticed him at all because of the snow, only that the trunks of the trees formed a darker background, against which his spotless apparel stood out plainly.

He looked greatly distressed at sight of the two boys. At first they thought he was figuring on running, but somehow the camp did not seem to offer him a safe asylum; and as for the woods he knew next to nothing about such a wilderness, since he had come from a city like New York.

So the chef compromised, as many a sensible man before him has found it profitable to do when confronted with a choice of evils; he elevated both his hands as if to let them know he surrendered unconditionally.

"Come on!" said Phil, on seeing this sign; "we'll ask him a few questions anyway."

They quickly joined the man in white. He was surveying the boys with a look of bewilderment on his pallid face.

"You do not look so terrible as heem!" they heard him say, in what might be considered a conciliatory tone.

"Who are you?" asked Phil, getting down to business at once.

"François Lavelle," came the prompt answer, as the chef drew himself up with a bit of perhaps unconscious pride.

"Are you Mr. Bodman's cook?" asked Ethan, curiously.

"I am ze French chef," he was instantly told, as though there might be a vast difference; "I haf serve him for five years; and he would not even come up to zis heathen country unless François he accompany heem to serve ze meals he adores."

"What has been going on over here? We heard all sorts of noises from our camp, as though there was murder being done; and so we've come across country to find out what it meant?"

When Phil said this the chef shivered, and drew up his shoulders in a ridiculous fashion that Ethan afterwards used to recall with shouts of laughter, it seemed so comical.

"If zere haf not been murder done," he said, solemnly, "it haf been because pouf! I run so fast. Begar! zat devil haf murder in hees eyes."

"Then the dog did go mad?" burst out Ethan wonderingly.

"Dog—mad?" stammered François, as though puzzled; "I do not understand. Eet is not ze dog zat go mad but zat terrible man who haf come to take my life!"

"Why should any one want to kill you?" asked Ethan; "did you forget to put seasoning in the soup; or was there too much cayenne pepper in the stew?"

"Parbleau! m'sieu, eet was all about ze hot water!"

"Please continue, because you have interested us very much," urged Phil; "what happened with the scalding water?"

"I threw zat same all over ze strange dog zat come into ze camp. On my honor I hold up zis hand and swear I zink it a savage wolf; so on ze impulse of ze minute pouf! and all over heem it goes!"

"Oh! now we are beginning to see a little light, François; when did this happen?" Phil continued, just as a lawyer cross-questioning a witness gradually succeeds in drawing out the entire story.

"Zis afternoon, m'sieu. Ze guides zey laugh, and say I am one hero; but zey also wink at each uzzer. I suspicion zey know who ze dog belong to, and believe zat I hear again from eet. Sacre! I did!"

"You mean the owner of the scalded dog came to your camp, and demanded satisfaction?" Phil asked.

"Zat ees what happened. He was a terror I am assuring you. My flesh seemed to grow cold like ze ice, when I hear him roar zat he haf come to demand ze satisfaction for ze injury to hees dog."

"Who did he say this to, François?"

"Who but ze master, M. Bodman heemself. Ze first zing I notice was zat both the brave guides zey haf zere hands held up in ze air, as eef to show zat it was none of zere affair."

"Wise men, François, and it looks as if they knew this visitor. Did you hear his name mentioned?"

"Oui, m'sieu. Eet was when my employer say heem Mr. James Bodman, and zat he is a power un ze world of finance; when zis pig owner of ze dog tell how he ees ze Terrible Badger, and zat he runs zings up here in the woods as he pleases."

"Then it seems that Mr. Bodman met his match at last. He was pretty hot about the collar, wasn't he, François; I mean, of course, that he acted furious?" Ethan asked.

"It did not make any deeference to zat Terrible Badger. He see ze dog zat was worth five hundred dollars, and with one shot from hees gun he kills heem."

"Whew! he must have been wild!" declared Ethan; "but we heard a lot of shooting and shouting, François; did the others of the party dare attack this man of the woods, and was there a regular battle?"

"I do not zink so, m'sieu. I myself am running evaire so fast just zen; but ze last look I take I have seen my employer dancing ze hop-step-and-jump while zat madman shoot close to hees toes."

Ethan could not keep a broad grin from appearing on his face at that.

"Then it must have been those two who were doing most of the shouting, the dancing man threatening all sorts of things that were to come; and the man with the gun telling him to try another step like the tango. You'd think, even if the guides washed their hands of the whole business, the other sportsmen might have taken a hand in the game, instead merely of looking on."

"Oh! zey did, I assure you, m'sieu! Zey dance just ze same as ze gentleman. Eet may be zat wild-man he tell zem zey must keep time wif ze music or ze bullets zey might not miss zere ankles."

"And so you were running off all this time, were you, François?" asked Phil, who no longer had any difficulty in understanding what it meant.

"What would you haf me do, m'sieu?" demanded the chef, indignantly; "I haf von wife and five charming children at home. Who support zem eef I allow myself to be sacrificed to ze passion of zat madman? I am of ze brave family over in France, but I am also not ze fool."

"And you managed to escape without him discovering you?" continued Phil.

"Aha! I slip in and out of ze trees. Heem so much taken up wif ze dance of ze gentlemen zat he nevaire see poor François. So I reach zis place and sink down to ze ground to recover my breath."

"But he went away finally, I suppose?" Phil questioned.

"After he haf exhaust ze gentlemen, and haf hees leetle joke."

"And no one lifted a hand to stay his departure, did they, François?"

"Ze guides would not, because zey haf to live up here in ze woods, and zey dare not make ze enemy of zat Terrible Badger. And ze three gentlemen could not walk over to ze cabin where zere guns were, zey were so exhausted."

"But that happened all of half an hour ago, didn't it, François?"

"I am not in ze condition to say, m'sieu. All I know is zat I haf not yet entirely recover from my knees knocking against each other; and as for my heart it keeps on jumping up into ze throat every time I hear a rustle close by. I zink zat man haf come back to get me, ze culprit, who is guilty of throwing ze boiling water on hees hound."

"But why haven't you gone back into the camp?" continued Ethan. "Surely it would be safer for you among those who have guns."

"Ah! m'sieu, it ees easy to talk, but you do not know how terrible zat wild man look. And if ze guides zey will not lift a hand to fight, what chance would poor François haf? I shall remain here in zis beautiful retreat till ze darkness come, and zen go back to make a new bargain with M. Bodman. Eef he promise to protect me I can again cook ze lofely meals; but eef he refuses me zat favor eet means zat François' skill ees lost. Everyzing I try I should make a failure of. Ze soup eet be spill, ze bread burned, and ze dishes he adores I forget how to make."

"Oh! the danger is likely all over with, François," Phil told the poor shivering chef. "This angry owner of the dogs has taken his revenge, and will fight shy of your camp after this. You can go back without running any great risk. But do you think any one was hurt by all that shooting?"

A negative shake of the head answered this question.

"But we only see one of the guides in the camp?" continued Phil.

"Ze gentlemen zey are in ze cabin resting after zere mad dance. Zey haf to keep eet up till zey nearly ready to drop before he say he haf enough. I am afraid zat M. Bodman he burst a blood vessel, he appear to be so red in hees face. Ze uzzer guide zey haf in zere doing somezings for zem."

Phil was completely satisfied by now.

"Nothing for us to do over here, it seems, Ethan," he suggested.

"I reckon not," replied the other.

"Our intentions were good, but fortunately there is no need of our services, as nobody was injured. So we might as well start back home, Ethan."

"Better take a picture of François here, with the camp for a background, Phil. Then you'll have something to show when you tell this story later on. And François wouldn't object, I should think?"

Phil seemed to think it would not be a bad idea.

"Those five tree trunks will make a good scene in themselves, with the snow, and the camp with its fire and smoke back of them. François, would you mind leaning out, and looking at me for just a few seconds?"

The chef was apparently an obliging sort of fellow; either that or else he had just experienced such a fright that he did not care to antagonize any more of the people he ran across up in this wilderness. He did as Phil requested, and the picture was taken in that fashion.

After that the boys bade him good-by, and turned their backs on the scene of the recent happening. Both of them felt well repaid for their short trip. They had learned what the loud commotion in the rival camp had meant; and were carrying back some mighty interesting news for the others.

Ethan was chuckling all the way.

"I just can't help but laugh at what that French cook told us," he remarked, as though he felt it really necessary to explain his actions. "Just imagine your fiery, red-faced, stout millionaire dancing furiously, while the owner of the scalded dog fires an occasional shot, cowboy fashion, close to his toes to make him jig faster. And all the while they are both yelling, the one in crazy delight and the other as mad as they make 'em. Oh! I'll burst my sides laughing yet."

"Well, it must have been a comical sight," admitted Phil, smiling broadly himself, "at least to an outsider, though I suppose those three men think it's an outrage serious enough to cause war between Uncle Sam and Canada right away after they get back home and report it."

"If only you had been right where we found the cook, Phil, with your camera, and cracked off a few shots of that dance, they'd be the best ever."

"Yes, that would have been a fine thing, but of course it couldn't ever be," the other continued. "But how about the man who was the cause of all this row; we ought to be able to guess who he was, without much trouble."

"François said he called himself the Terrible Badger!"

"Allowing for François being badly frightened we can put our interpretation on that," said Phil. "Instead of Badger say Baylay, and you've got it straight."

"Whew! both that logger and Mr. McNab did say he was an awful case, didn't they? And seems like all men are alike to him. Little he cares whether it's an American millionaire railroad wrecker, or just a plain sportsman, Anson Baylay snaps his fingers and tells them to dance, and they do dance."

"He might choose to treat us the same way, so don't crow too loud, Ethan," warned the other.

"What! after we've done so much for his kid that has the impediment in his speech? I should think he'd have some kind of gratitude about him. But if this was Baylay somehow he didn't seem to mention anything about losing a child, that François heard?"

"It may be he hasn't been home for several days," explained Phil. "I understand he carried a line of traps somewhere up here; and possibly he is compelled to be away for days at a time. But he must have been on the way home when his dog got that scalding at the hands of the French cook, who thought it was a bold wolf invading the camp."

"Then if Baylay gets home this afternoon or evening he's likely to hear about his terrible loss. In that case we may expect to see him within the next twenty-four hours, wouldn't you think, Phil?"

"If he doesn't show up by to-morrow morning I plan to start out and try to find his cabin, so we can let them know we have the boy safe and sound. But here we are close on our camp, and everything seems to be serene there."

CHAPTER XV — THE FIRE VIGIL

When the sound of their snow-shoes crunching over the surface of the drifts came to the ears of Lub, still seated there on the log, he was seen to start, and half raise his gun, while he evidently gave some sort of signal, for X-Ray came rushing out of the shack, also armed.

At discovering that there was no sudden peril both the defenders of the camp laughed at their fears.

"Welcome back, fellows!" sang out Lub; "didn't expect you so soon, and supper is not even started yet. But after we've heard your report we'll get busy."

"Did you go all the way over?" asked X-Ray, eagerly.

"We sure did," replied Ethan.

"And perhaps now you learned what the row was about?" continued Lub.

"They were having a dance," said Ethan, with a suggestive grin.

"It must have been because they were half drunk, then," sneered X-Ray.

"Nope; perfectly sober, so far as we could learn from their chef. You see, Mr. Bodman and his two sportsmen guests were coaxed to dance against their will. Every time a gun went off, and the bullet kicked up the snow and dirt near their feet they had to jump all the harder!"

Of course it was Ethan's object to arouse the wonder of the other pair, and to judge from the puzzled expression on their faces he had already succeeded in doing so.

"Oh! come on, and tell us all about it," said Lub.

At that the two returned scouts found places on the log, and started to relate how they had come upon the panic-stricken chef, who by degrees had told the whole remarkable happening, beginning with his mistake in scalding a stray dog under the impression that it was a prowling wolf, down to the minute they came upon him hiding there, and afraid to go back to the camp lest he be confronted with that furious giant of a woodsman, wild to avenge the insult to his four-footed pet.

Never had Lub and X-Ray listened to a more curious and thrilling story. They almost held their very breath as they hung upon every word, with a look of intense interest stamped on their faces.

"Now," said Phil, when everything they had learned had been told, "what do you two think about it? Was the Terrible Badger the man we've been hearing so much about since coming up here—Baylay?"

"Must be that he is," announced X-Ray, promptly.

"Well, the indications all point that way," Lub remarked, in his slow fashion, as though he might be still weighing things in his mind. "There are so few persons up around here that it couldn't well be any one else. So we'll have to take it for granted the owner of the dog is Baylay."

"Hurra! since Lub has finally figured it out the rest of us needn't bother about it any more. Lub has settled the thing beyond all dispute," laughed Ethan.

"Well, I guess you'll find that I'm right," ventured Lub, who often took himself very seriously, and in this way sometimes intensified the joke.

"How about that grub, chef?" asked Ethan; "that little tramp seems to have put an edge on my appetite."

"Huh! as if it wasn't always sharp enough," Lub told him; "but if there's nothing more to listen to I suppose I might as well get busy. You see, I've got a pot of beans cooking there, which has been on more'n two hours, so I should think the things would be fairly done. And along with that we're going to have some fried ham, with eggs to follow, coffee, cakes, and then crackers and cheese for those who feel that way."

"Well, if it will hurry things up any I'm ready to pitch in and help you, chef," Ethan told him.

"Get some more wood, then!" ordered Lub, "and be careful about that bean-pot. I hung it across on that iron rod from two stakes with crotches on top, but it is a little shaky. If you spill the beans your name will be Dennis, I warn you."

"He'd better cut a hole in the ice and drown himself if he's that clumsy," warned X-Ray; "for after smelling those beans cooking all this time it would make me pretty cross if I was cheated out of having three messes for supper."

Somehow even tender-hearted Lub had not been heard to express anything like sorrow on account of what had happened over at the other camp. In fact all of them seemed to be of the one mind; and to think that it served the bossy millionaire about right to be ordered around a little, and made to dance a hornpipe at the dictation of the terror of the pine woods.

According to their notion it was a dose of his own medicine Mr. James Bodman had been compelled to take. No doubt many a time he had by his brutal methods of frenzied finance compelled others to dance to his fiddling; and now he knew how it felt himself.

Indeed, X-Ray was filled with only one keen regret. He would have given almost anything for the pleasure of being in position to see what the Frenchchef had so aptly described.

"Just to think of that red-faced fat old fellow dancing as the bullets plowed up the snow close to his toes!" he was heard to say; "I can see him jumping up and down like mad, cracking his heels together, puffing like a winded nag, and screaming his threats at the man who was treating him as if he were only a common every-day ten dollar a week clerk, instead of the great American millionaire. Wow! it must have been rich, though!"

They could talk of nothing else all evening. No matter what subject was broached some one was sure to bring it back to the one intensely interesting topic.

It seemed to be the consensus of opinion among them that Phil was right when he figured that Baylay could not have been home before he visited the other camp. If he had known of his child's vanishing in the great snow forest he would hardly have bothered himself seeking revenge for the injury to his dog. On the contrary it was more than likely he would have besought the inmates of the camp to come to his assistance in trying to find the child, even though all hope of the little one being still alive must be abandoned.

"I wonder if we will see him here, sooner or later?" Lub ventured to say, and then giving his little charge a benevolent look he continued: "If he could only up and tell us things it'd make it so much easier. Sometimes seems to me the boy knows what I'm saying to him, and tries the best he can to answer, but as yet I haven't mastered his sign language. Chances are his mammy would know everything he wants to tell."

"He's gone to sleep now," remarked Phil, "after that fine supper he put away. One thing sure, he hasn't lost his appetite even if he has his folks."

"Can you blame the little shaver?" said Lub, quickly; "like as not it's been a long spell since he's seen such grub as we put before him, and plenty of it at that. Up here the guides are in the habit of taking what they call pot-luck; one day plenty of meat on hand, and another time the pot is pretty nearly empty."

"X-Ray, don't you want to come out with me for a short time?" asked Phil as he got on his feet.

"Sure I do," the other replied, without the slightest hesitation in his manner or speech; "what's doing now, Phil?"

"Oh! you remember I said I had found several places where certain small fur-bearing animals live. An old trapper would say they 'use' the ground where their tracks show. Well, I want to get some flashlight pictures of the same, and it's to lay my trap that I'm going out now."

"Glad you don't think of going alone, Phil," remarked Lub, seriously.

"Why, do you think I might run up against a wolf pack, and have to climb a tree to save myself from their teeth?" laughed Phil, as he slung the camera over his shoulder, and then picked up his repeating rifle.

"Well, it wasn't so much that as the chance of your meeting some of the ugly crowd from the other camp that made me say what I did," Lub continued. "Any lot of people who could get down so low as to try and burn a party of boys out of their shack, just for petty spite, would be capable of doing pretty nearly anything."

At that both Phil and Ethan laughed loudly.

"Make your mind easy about that millionaire and his party!" exclaimed the latter, "they've had enough experience with the Terrible Baylay to do them a life-time. I rather think they'll be afraid to venture far away from their old camp the rest of the time they're up here. Fact is, it wouldn't surprise me a whit if they packed up and vacated inside of twenty-four hours."

"And you're saying just what was in my mind, too, Ethan," Phil added. "Not one of those three wealthy men could be tempted to get away from the fire this night; and I rather think they'll take a dislike to the whole neighborhood. They haven't been very lucky since coming here."

"Not in getting their caribou, anyway," said X-Ray, uproariously, as he allowed his thoughts to go back to the time when he and Phil offered their leavings to the domineering financier, after he tried to make out he had first claim to the quarry that had been brought down.

As Phil had made all his preparations beforehand they experienced little difficulty in placing the trap. It was so arranged that the mink could not possibly get the attractive bait without setting the flashlight cartridge off; and if everything worked well his picture would be taken as neatly as though the photographer were present in person to superintend things.

"I hope this will be the beginning of a series of successful jobs along this same line," Phil was saying, as after arranging things to suit his ideas they headed in the direction of camp once more.

"You haven't given up the idea of visiting that beaver settlement, I hope, Phil?"

"Just as soon as we get the boy off our hands we'll take it up," he was told.

"While that is hanging over us I'd rather stay near home; because whether Baylay comes in the dead of night, or by the light of the sun I want to be there to meet him."

"And the rest of us would rather have it that way, I'm sure," admitted Ethan, which was enough in itself to show how the balance of the Mountain Boys had come to depend on Phil as their leader. "But if you feel so sure none of that crowd will venture out to-night, is that going to make any change in our regular program of keeping watch, Phil?"

"No, I don't see why it should," came the ready response. "It's a good habit to get into, and the more we practice it the better we can stand our stint without feeling like going to sleep on post."

"I half expect you're looking for a visit from Baylay," ventured Ethan, shrewdly.

"That depends a good deal on whether he knows about our being here," he was told.

"If he didn't happen to see our smoke, or run across McNab when the farmer was getting out of the bush, of course he wouldn't be apt to come this way. In that event the man would spend all his time scouting the snow woods around the place where we picked up the kid."

"He must be a smart tracker, Phil?"

"It stands to reason that he is," replied the other; "and I can give a good guess why you say that, Ethan. You think he may try to follow the boy from the time he started out, with his little popgun under his arm, just as he had seen his daddy go forth many a time on a hunt for fresh meat."

"If he did, and the wind hasn't drifted the dry snow so as to cover the trail all up, why in the course of time he'd reach the spot where we found the kid; and as the trail ended there he might guess somebody had found him, or else the wolves had carried the boy off."

"That's true enough, Ethan; but as the wind has been blowing more or less ever since, and the snow is like powder, I'm afraid that trail of the boy has been covered long ago. Even the smartest tracker couldn't keep it long. But we'll have to wait and see what turns up."

They sat there before the fire for a long time. There was so much to talk about that the time passed before they knew it. Lub had some while since managed to get his little charge tucked away under the capacious blanket, and he now declared his intention of joining him.

Phil insisted upon taking the first watch on this particular night, and while the other pair may have had some idea as to what his reason was they did not ask any questions.

"You'll wake me in good time, remember, Phil," had been the last words of X-Ray as he smothered a tremendous yawn; and then followed Ethan under his blanket.

Phil sat there watching the fire, which he meant to keep burning cheerfully all through his time on guard. If any one were heading for the camp through the snow woods that welcome pyramid of flame would serve as a guidepost to their steps. And somehow Phil seemed to have the utmost confidence that sooner or later his vigilance would be rewarded.

An hour, two of them almost had passed, and beyond the customary noises of the night nothing had broken upon his hearing. The wind murmured and fretted among the pine-tops; or a limb creaked mournfully as it scraped across another. A snow owl called to its mate in the deeper recesses of the woods; perhaps some daring little creatures came creeping from unknown recesses under various roots, and hunted for crumbs of food near the camp.

Then Phil raised his head to listen. He smiled, and nodded, as though satisfied his long vigil was about to be rewarded.

Yes, plainly now he caught the peculiar crunch of advancing snow-shoes. The sound came from the quarter away from the lake; and it was in that direction they believed the waif's people had their lonely cabin, deep in the recesses of the bush, so that only with the greatest difficulty could any venturesome game warden ever find the home of the poacher who scorned all their warnings, and defied arrest.

Nearer the sounds came. Whoever it was advancing he was apparently in a desperate hurry; and that seemed to fit in with Phil's way of figuring. Indeed, with the fate of that little darling of a boy hung up in the balance he could not see how any father who cared at all for his child would linger on the snow-shoe trail.

Phil arose quietly to his feet. The sounds were close at hand as a huge form loomed up in the light of the firelight; and Phil drew a breath of relief as he realized that the crisis had come; for that could be no other than the poacher Baylay, come to ask in his anguish if they had seen the lost boy.

CHAPTER XVI — BAYLAY'S HOME-COMING — CONCLUSION

As Phil stood there, he saw the big man who had terrorized the Bodman camp so recently, swiftly advance.

There was no evidence of braggadocio about Baylay now. He had a gun in his hand, but this he held up as though to let those in the camp understand that he came in peace.

Phil wanted the other to show his colors. Great was his amazement when he caught a half-choked appealing emotion in the other's tones. Evidently all the fight had been suddenly taken from Anson Baylay when he arrived home and learned of his terrible loss.

"I'm acomin' to ask ye to help me," he started to say. "I can't find him in the snow; an' ma says p'raps somebody might a picked him up. I hopes so, sure, 'cause we sets a store by the kid. Hev ye seen my Kinney?"

"Are you the man they call the Terrible Baylay?" asked Phil.

"Anson Baylay is my name, but I ain't so terrible; seein' I feel as weak as a cat, 'cause o' this thing that's happened; an' wi' ma acryin' her head off. But ye ain't tole me yit if ye seen a sign o' my lettle boy Kinney. Tell me the wost, stranger; I kin stand it; but I sure hate to fetch the news hum to her."

"Is Kinney a little boy with yellow hair and blue eyes?" asked Phil.

"Yes, yes, that's him!" gasped the giant, thrusting out a trembling hand and gripping the boy by the arm so that Phil winced.

"Don't squeeze my arm like that, Baylay," he said, hastily; "you may not mean to hurt but all the same you do. Tell me, is Kinney tongue-tied, so that he can't say a word?"

"That's what he is, mister; but the dearest little cub as ever was born! Does you mean to tell me ye seen him?" cried Baylay.

"Kinney's safe and sound, Baylay, and I guess that's the best news you ever had," Phil hastened to say, for he saw that the man was suffering tortures in his hopes and fears.

122

With that the giant gave a sigh that must have welled up from his heart. "Is he here with ye, mister?" he managed to ask, tremulously.

"He's sound asleep in our shack here," said Phil; "we ran on him in the woods. He had gone out hunting, with his little popgun. When he found himself lost and getting very cold the brave little chap tried the best he knew how to start a fire, but the deep snow kept him from finding the right sort of kindling. He had given up when we ran across him, attracted by his moaning. But we came up just in time."

"Take me to him, mister, please take me to him. I can't believe it 'less I see him, and 'less I feel him. I sure thought he was gone away from us forever. And my heart is ahungerin' for Kinney. We got other kids, but there be only one Kinney!"

Phil could not resist. He knew the big logger would have rushed into the shack anyway, even if he had declined to wake the others up.

"Wait here, and I'll fetch the boy," he said.

First he threw on some more wood, so that the fire would start afresh. Then, entering he bent over each of his comrades, saying:

"Wake up, and come out; he's here!"

As Lub started to crawl from under his blanket Phil reached over and picking up the now wideawake little lad he said close to his ear:

"Daddy's come for you, Kinney; he's outside here waiting to hug you!"

They all came tumbling out in a bunch, eager to witness the meeting between their little ward and his terrible father.

When Lub saw the man fiercely hugging the little mite, with the child's arms pressed around his neck, he stood there staring, and Phil heard him say to himself wonderingly:

"And they call that big-hearted man the Terrible Baylay, do they? Well, I guess after all he's only a bluff, and just the same as any other fellow. Why, honest to goodness I do believe there are real tears rolling down his cheeks right now."

But Phil knew it was the power of love making this giant as a child.

"You must stay the rest of the night with us," he told the giant, "and in the morning some of us will go with you to your cabin. We want to meet the mother of the boy, because we've got something to propose that will be a blessing to you and to Kinney."

At first Baylay wanted to carry the good news to the mother. But Phil told him he must consider the boy.

Then Baylay thought of going alone to take the joyful tidings to the grieving heart in that lonely cabin; but he lacked the nerve to tear himself away from the little chap whose arms were about his big neck and whose kisses were pressing on his bearded cheek.

Consequently he finally agreed to remain, and since sleep would doubtless refuse to come to any of them during the balance of that eventful night they sat there by the fire and talked.

Phil believed he knew of a plan whereby a certain cherished scheme of his own could be put through, with Baylay as the manager of the farm on which Phil meant to try and breed the valuable silver black foxes, with their pelts worth fortunes.

He even mentioned this to the former guide, trapper, and logger, and discovering that Baylay was fully posted as to every detail, Phil made a proposition to him, which was joyfully accepted.

When morning came Lub had plenty of assistance in getting a hurried breakfast, and that finished they prepared to start forth.

However, in due time the whole party managed to reach the isolated cabin where Anson Baylay lived.

When they saw little Kinney safe in the arms of his mother, who was almost wild with joy, it was noticeable how each of the boys found it necessary to turn aside and wink violently as they pretended to be looking at something which had suddenly attracted their attention.

As they sat at the homely table in that cabin and the face of the poacher's happy wife beamed with smiles, Phil gently took up the other subject.

When those parents learned that there was a strong possibility of an operation giving their afflicted child the blessed power of speech; and that these splendid boys offered to stand all the expense, taking Kinney and his mother with them to Montreal for the occasion, they could not find words to express the deep gratitude that filled their hearts.

So it was settled, and when the time came for the Mountain Boys to depart the Baylay family would go with them to civilization, where Anson could keep in touch with his new employer from time to time. Then the mother and Kinney would accompany Phil and his chums as far as Montreal.

Phil managed to get his striking picture of a great bull moose; and Ethan on his part shot the monster later on, so that he could have the horns as a trophy of his skill.

They no longer saw Mr. James Bodman and his party, as the Saguenay River country had become too unpleasant for them.

Finally Tammis McNab came with his sledge and ponies. It was crowding matters to take them all, but he landed them safely at the town, where they could be transported to the St. Lawrence.

In due time the boys arrived in Montreal with Mrs. Baylay and Kinney. A famous surgeon told them there would be no difficulty whatever in performing a successful operation; and that inside of a few months no one would ever know the child had had any difficulty in enunciating.

"Well," said Lub, when with his three chums he made himself comfortable in the Pullman car at the Montreal station, and were about to enter upon the last lap of the homeward journey; "I kind of think this has been the most remarkable of all our trips. And I wonder where the next one will take us."

"Nobody can say just now," laughed Phil. "Our vacation is near an end, and we'll soon be hard at work again; but no matter where the Mountain Boys go they know how to take care of themselves."

In this happy mood, then, did Phil and his chums go back to their homes in Brewster, satisfied that they had a glorious time during their snow-shoe trip to the wilds of Canada, and not regretting for a single minute they had undertaken the long journey.

It was to be expected that the Mountain Boys would enjoy other outings of a similar character; and the author only hopes it will be his pleasing duty to chronicle their doings for the benefit of the many young friends who have followed their fortunes through the pages of this and the preceding books of the series.

THE END